He Was Rough And Tough, Brash And Bold As Only A True Cowboy, One Who'd Grown Up In The Life, Could Be.

Sure, there was no denying that he was also wildly gorgeous. He knew it, too, bone deep, like a baby knows one dimple-cheeked and drooling grin could turn the most stoic skeptic into a babbling idiot.

He'd been described as one of those men who oozed confidence and competence—and wore both in a way that made men respect him and women wonder what it would take to tame him.

Well, *some* women at any rate. She just didn't happen to be one of them.

At least she didn't want to be.

Dear Reader,

Silhouette Desire is starting the New Year off with a bang as we introduce our brand-new family-centric continuity, DYNASTIES: THE ASHTONS. Set in the lush wine-making country of Napa Valley, California, the Ashtons are a family divided by a less-than-fatherly patriarch. We think you'll be thoroughly entranced by all the drama and romance when the wonderful Eileen Wilks starts things off with *Entangled*. Look for a new book in the series each month…all year long.

The New Year also brings new things from the fabulous Dixie Browning as she launches DIVAS WHO DISH. You'll love her sassy heroine in *Her Passionate Plan B*. SONS OF THE DESERT, Alexandra Sellers's memorable series, is back this month with the dramatic conclusion, *The Fierce and Tender Sheikh*. RITA® Award-winning author Cindy Gerard will thrill you with the heart-stopping hero in *Between Midnight and Morning*. (My favorite time of the night. What about you?)

Rounding out the month are two clever stories about shocking romances: Shawna Delacorte's tale of a sexy hero who falls for his best friend's sister, *In Forbidden Territory*, and Shirley Rogers's story of a secretary who ends up winning her boss in a bachelor auction, *Business Affairs*.

Here's to a New Year's resolution we should all keep: indulging in more *desire!*

Happy reading,

Melissa Jeglinski

Melissa Jeglinski
Senior Editor, Silhouette Desire

Please address questions and book requests to:
Silhouette Reader Service
U.S.: 3010 Walden Ave., P.O. Box 1325, Buffalo, NY 14269
Canadian: P.O. Box 609, Fort Erie, Ont. L2A 5X3

Between Midnight and Morning

Cindy Gerard

Silhouette® Desire

Published by Silhouette Books

America's Publisher of Contemporary Romance

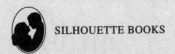 SILHOUETTE BOOKS

ISBN 0-373-76630-0

BETWEEN MIDNIGHT AND MORNING

Copyright © 2005 by Cindy Gerard.

This edition published by arrangement with Harlequin Books S.A.

Visit Silhouette Books at www.eHarlequin.com

Printed in U.S.A.

CINDY GERARD

Since her first release in 1991 hit the national #1 slot on the Waldenbooks bestseller list, Cindy Gerard has repeatedly made appearances on several bestseller lists, including *USA TODAY*.

With numerous industry awards to her credit—among them the Romance Writers of America's RITA® Award and the National Reader's Choice Award—this former Golden Heart finalist and repeat *Romantic Times* nominee is the real deal. As one book reviewer put it, "Cindy Gerard provides everything romance readers want in a love story—passion, gut-wrenching emotion, intriguing characters and a captivating plot. This storyteller extraordinaire delivers all of this and more!"

Cindy and her husband, Tom, live in the Midwest on a minifarm with quarter horses, cats and two very spoiled dogs. When she's not writing, she enjoys reading, traveling and spending time at their cabin in northern Minnesota unwinding with family and friends. Cindy loves to hear from her readers and invites you to visit her Web site at www.cindygerard.com.

To Kayla and Blake—
you are all things good and wonderful.

One

He ought to get down in the dirt beside her. That would be the *right* thing to do. But the *fun* thing was to watch the good doctor try to wrestle the brindle calf into submission.

Yeah, the right thing would be to help her out because she was definitely going down for the count. But she *had* told him to stay back, he reasoned. And the view of Alison Samuels's tidy little backside looked mighty fine from where he stood. *Mighty fine.*

John Tyler thumbed back his Resistol and hitched a dusty boot on the bottom rail of his dry lot fence. Crossing his arms over the top board, he settled in to watch the show…and a fine one it was proving to be, he thought with a grin.

Damn, the doc was a tiny little thing. Cute as a button, too, with her honey-blond hair pulled back in a long animated ponytail. Like her, it had looked sleek and professional when she'd answered his call this morning. It didn't look that way now. Nothing about her did. Now, she was a pretty, dirty mess. Despite the dust smearing cheeks pinkened with heat and exertion and flyaway strands of spun gold hair standing every which direction around her face, she was the kind of mess that made a man think of sweaty sheets, sultry sighs and a whole lot of pleasure between midnight and morning.

He straightened, cleared his throat and tugged his hat lower on his brow to cut the glare of the July sun. Then he told himself to think about something besides Alison Samuels's slim, bare limbs tangled with his. Something like why a city woman would want to pick up and move from Kansas City to Sundown, Montana, and take over old Doc Sebring's vet practice. And why this particular woman—who looked more predisposed to cocktail parties and little black dresses than wrestling with livestock—would make the choice to set up shop in what most folks referred to as north of nowhere, was as intriguing as hell.

It was almost as intriguing as her skintight Wranglers that strained at the seams while she hunkered down, dug her boot heels into the packed dirt, and tried to muscle the calf into her way of thinking. It wasn't gonna happen. Not with that technique. In fact, it was pretty apparent that up until this point in her vet career the biggest thing she'd ever wrestled was most likely a fat tabby with a hairball.

The brindle—a good one hundred fifty pounds of ornery on the hoof—let out a P.O.'d bellow, swung his head around and butted her under the chin. John winced then shook his head. Oh, man. That had to hurt like blazes. He'd been on the receiving end of one of those head butts. It was a pretty good bet that Doctor Dish was riding a rising tide of nausea and counting a sea of stars—but she gritted her teeth and hung on like a bull-dogger bent on winning a championship rodeo buckle.

Grit. She had it in spades. She couldn't hide the pain in her eyes, though, and when he saw it, he swore under his breath and decided this was as far as he was willing to let this fiasco go.

He swung himself up and over the fence, finessed the calf into a headlock and threw him on his side.

"Didn't ask for your help." The doc grunted, a little breathless, as she tugged the plastic cap off a syringe with her teeth and quickly jabbed the antibiotic into the wriggling animal's neck.

"And you obviously didn't need it." John tossed her a congenial grin as he released the calf. "But I just couldn't stand the idea of you having all that fun by yourself."

He rose to his feet then brushed corral grime off his jeans. Silver-blue eyes set in a face that made him think of porcelain and princesses met his through the heat and the dust as the calf ran, bawling, toward his anxious mother.

Judging by the look in her eyes, the doc was considering getting huffy. In the end, she just shook her head and gave up a weary grin.

"Well…far be it from me to spoil a boy's fun." She capped the needle, tossed it into her utility bucket and offered, if not an exuberant, an appreciative but weary, "Thanks."

Maybe it was the *boy* comment. Maybe it was her valiant defiance even after the calf had gained the upper hand. Or it could be it was just the pleasure of finally seeing her smile—even if it was a feeble effort. He was a sucker for a beautiful woman's smile, and this woman's had him asking a question he'd pretty much decided he wasn't going to ask her again.

"How about you thank me by having dinner with me tonight?"

She didn't even blink as she gathered up her supplies and headed for her truck, rinsed her hands in a bucket of soapy water then hastily dried them on a towel. After digging around in a refrigerated compartment in the vet unit topping the pickup box, she found what she wanted then filled two syringes with antibiotic.

"He'll need another dose tomorrow and one the day after," she said, handing him the medication. "If you don't see any improvement by midweek next week, give me a call."

John slipped the syringes into his shirt pocket. "Can do. Now…about dinner?"

Pointedly ignoring his question, she stowed her medical supplies, shut the compartment and skirted around him toward the truck's cab. "Have a good day, John," she said, climbing behind the wheel.

He caught the door before she could shut it, then stood in the opening, grinning up at her.

"It's J.T. My friends call me J.T."

She scowled down at him. "I need to get going."

Damn, she was something. Sweat streaked down her temple, corral grime powdered her cheeks. Her hair clung to her face and neck in wet ringlets and double damn, a bluish pink bruise had started forming just under the point of her chin.

Yeah. Even wrecked, she was something. And worth the rejection—six times by his last count since she'd set up shop in Sundown a month ago.

"Better get some ice on that," he suggested, pointing an index finger to his own chin.

"First chance I get."

Which meant never, if he read her tone right.

"Hold on. I'll get you an ice pack."

"You don't need to do that."

"I do," he insisted. "Sit tight."

He headed for the tack room in the barn before she could finish her protest. After finding a disposable pack in the freezer—bruises and sprains were standard fare on a working cattle ranch—he walked back to her truck.

"Thanks," she said again, and again with a grudging reluctance when he handed her the pack.

"You can thank me by going to dinner with me. Hey—how about that? Déjà vu all over again."

She made an exasperated sound. "What is it with you? Why do you bother? You know what the answer's going to be."

"Oh, it's that fun factor again, I suppose."

"I was thinking more along the lines of the hardhead factor."

He tugged on his earlobe, grinned. "That, too. I'm persistent as hell when something's important to me."

"And it's important that I go out to dinner with you? Why? I don't get it."

"Lord above, woman. Don't you ever look in a mirror?"

Their eyes met for the briefest of moments while the sun beat down like an endless lick from a bass guitar. Pulsing, heavy, hot.

She let out a huge sigh. "This is all very flattering. You're a sweet guy—"

"Good-looking, too," he pointed out, pleased as punch when that little bit of foolishness pried a small, reluctant grin out of her.

"And let's not forget humble," she added with a shake of her head. "But I'm not—"

"Interested. I know. Okay…so don't think of it as a date. Put any spin on it you want. Think of it as a neighbor being neighborly.

"Look," he continued reasonably, "you're single. I'm single. You have to eat. I have to eat. What part's hanging you up?"

She turned the key in the ignition, gripped the steering wheel with both hands and met his eyes with unwavering resolve. "It's not going to happen." Another sigh. A big one. "If you want to use another vet, I'll understand."

He waved that notion away and squinted up at her. "Is it the age thing? Because if it is—"

"Stop!" She dropped her forehead on the steering wheel with a groan. "It has nothing to do with our age difference."

"Well then, there you go." So he was thirty-two and she was forty—this tidbit of info compliments of his friend Peg Reno who was chummy with the doc. He didn't see a problem. She did, though, no matter that she claimed otherwise.

"Come on, Doc," he wheedled, trying his damnedest not to sound like he was doing just that. "We're talking about dinner, for Pete's sake. I'm not asking you to go to bed with me."

She lifted a brow and pinned him with a look that said, *aren't you?*

Yeah. Well. She had him there. He scratched his jaw. Eventually, hell yes, that's exactly where he wanted her. And as their gazes locked then held, he saw something in her eyes that punched him in the chest like a bullet. For an unexpected and sensually charged moment, cool blue accusation transitioned to awareness to heated longing…then to panic and desperate denial.

If he hadn't been paying attention, he'd have missed the whole parade because in the next instant, she shifted into gear, tore out the lane and laid a trail of Montana dust that boiled up behind her truck like a cyclone bent on rearranging hell's half acre.

And as he stood there, watching her go, he finally understood.

"Well, I'll be damned," he uttered under his breath and headed back for the barn. She wanted the same thing he did—which was a lot more than dinner—but for some reason, it scared her half to death.

Scared her and, inexplicably, made her sad. Yeah, he'd seen that in her eyes too, he realized as he opened the tack room door. The woman was a whole boatload of contradictions and complications…which begged the obvious question, why *was* he bothering?

Because the doc was a knockout, that's why.

Snagging Snowy's bridle, blanket and saddle, he headed for his mare's stall. Alison Samuels was sexy, intelligent, mature—unlike many of the women who came on to him—and he was guessing she'd be great in bed. Plus, everything about her suggested that she wouldn't probe or analyze or want to get all touchy-feely with his emotions or his life. Another major draw, he thought, sobering and walked into the stall with a soft "Hey, girl, time to earn your oats."

He set aside the tack, then tugged a brush out of his hip pocket. While he worked on the mare's coat, he thought about Alison's blue eyes that brought to mind Russian sage and sleepy mornings after. Eyes that always looked guarded and distant…a sure sign that she'd respect his privacy.

And privacy was something that grew more important to him with each passing day. Just like every day, he fought to keep from taking a wrong step and falling into the black hole that persisted in trying to take over his life. Most days, he won the battle. But some days…some days he didn't have it in him to even show up for the war.

Those were the days he wasn't fit to be around anyone. Those were the days he wasn't fit to *be*. On the best of the bad days, he'd saddle Snowy and try to outrun the darkness. On the worst, he'd hole up in his bedroom. Shades drawn, lights off. And wait to feel human again. Wait to be able to cope again. And feel like the weakest slug on earth because he had no control over when or how hard the darkness hit him.

Post-Traumatic Stress Disorder. That's what the marine shrinks called it. A result of his experiences in the field. It had been over two years ago. He'd wanted to be a warrior. He wanted to be on the front line where he could make a difference, so he fudged on his aptitude tests so they wouldn't stick him behind a desk working computers. Well, he'd made it to the front line all right but with a hospital field kit instead of a rifle. They'd made him a medic. And he'd forever be haunted by what he'd seen and done.

Yeah, they called it PTSD. He called it something else. Weakness. And his inability to lick it filled him with shame. So much shame that he hid it. Hid it from his friends, hid it from his family. Sometimes, for weeks at a time, he even managed to hide it from himself.

Hell, ask anyone who knew him and they'd tell you the same thing. *John Tyler? He was one good-time Charlie. Nothing gets to J.T. Always grinning. Always flirting with the ladies. A wild one, that boy, and pity the woman who ever expects him to settle down.*

Well, no woman was ever going to have to worry about that. Because no woman deserved to be saddled with him for the long haul. The minute a woman showed signs of wanting more from him than a good time and a hot physical relationship, he was gone. If they started telling him their life stories, then they'd expect the same from him and that just wasn't going to happen. The last thing he wanted was a long-term relationship and the inherent emotional intimacy that went with the territory.

Which led him right back to Alison. He strongly suspected that the blond doc had secrets, too. Her eyes told him that much. She had something in her past she either wanted to forget or keep under lock and key. He didn't want to know about it, just as he was guessing she wouldn't want to know about his.

"What do you think, pretty girl?" he murmured, scratching the bald-faced sorrel's jaw. "Seems to me she's just what the doctor ordered. An independent woman who won't feel the need to fix me or get too deeply involved."

Snowy stood placidly while he settled a saddle blanket over her back.

"Could you be a little more decisive?" he continued and hefted the saddle high on her withers. "No? Well, guess I'll just have to go with my gut on this then."

As he led Snowy out of the barn into the sunlight, his gut told him maybe a fight's what he needed—a challenge with a reward at the end instead of merely relief for making it through another day. The doc was definitely a challenge—and a reward.

He mounted the mare and headed for the summer pasture, looking forward to the long ride ahead of him. A ride long enough to come up with any number of ways to win the doc over to his way of thinking. If nothing else, it would keep his mind from wandering back to the black.

Two

"I don't know." Weary to the bone, Ali sat on the top tread of her front porch steps. She glanced at Peg Reno who sat beside her, then stared beyond the quiet street toward the wild mountain range rising west of town where an apricot orange sun was slowly sinking out of sight. "Sometimes this feels like the biggest mistake of my life."

Rather than meet Peg's concerned gaze, Ali averted her attention to the sweating glass of iced tea she cupped between her hands. Even though theirs was a new friendship, the bond she and Peg had forged during the past month was solid. When Peg sighed, Ali heard understanding and support. Peg's words punctuated both.

"What you're dealing with here is a sneaky case of buyer's remorse. And I'm not talking about buying Doc Sebring's vet practice."

"Don't be too sure about that. Kitties and hamsters generally don't leave bruises." Ali gingerly touched the tender bruise on her chin—compliments of her new vet practice and the hit she'd taken from John Tyler's calf earlier this afternoon.

"Look," Peg said, unfolding her long, slim legs. She rose, walked down the five steps, then stood at the bottom and met Ali eye for eye. "You've had a tough day. You've made one adjustment after another in the last month, what with moving out here, setting up the practice and getting used to an entirely different kind of clientele. But my guess is that it's not the business giving you trouble. It's the idea that you're not in Kansas anymore, Dorothy— and that's what's got you second-guessing yourself."

Ali glanced down one of barely four-dozen streets that made up Sundown, the tiny Montana town she now called home—except it sure didn't feel like home. Peg was right. She wasn't anywhere near Kansas or, more literally and in the local vernacular, she was a *far piece* from Kansas City, where she'd spent the last several years of her life after growing up in Chicago. She was a city girl down to the soles of her dusty size six work boots and Sundown, well, Sundown, was *not* a city.

She dragged a hand through her hair and glanced up to meet Peg's sympathetic look. With her waist-length curtain of straight chestnut hair, honey-brown eyes and unbelievably lush and long body packed in cut-off jeans and a flame-red tank top, Peg could have been a Victoria's Secret model. Yet here she was. She'd grown up in Sundown. Lived and loved her hunky bronc rider hubby, Cutter Reno, in Sundown, was raising her family in Sundown and would likely end her days here in Sundown.

"How do you do it?"

"It? Now you're getting personal," Peg teased with a wicked waggle of her brows.

Okay, Ali conceded with a grin. If she shared a bed with a man like Cutter Reno, her thoughts would be channeled in that direction, too. But she didn't share a bed with anyone, hadn't since David died four years ago, and regardless of John Tyler's repeated and open invitation, she wasn't going to.

"You know what I mean, Mrs. Reno," she said to her friend.

"Yeah." Grinning, too, Peg stuffed her fingers into the back pockets of her shorts. "I know what you mean." She sobered, lifted a shoulder. "And I imagine I'd have just as hard of a time adjusting to the city as you're having adjusting to life out here. Give it some time. It'll grow on you. Yeah, it's quiet. Yeah, it's slow. But there's something special about that, you know? Forces a person to make more out of less. Sometimes, that can be a good thing.

"And speaking of good things," Peg added as Ali thought about what she said, "heard you got called out to J.T.'s again today. What's that—seven or eight times this month?"

"Six…and how do you hear these things?"

"Small-town grapevine. So…did he hit on you again?"

Ali snorted before downing another swallow of tea. "Does a cow have hide?"

Peg chuckled. "Is he making any headway?"

"*Peg.* Don't start on me about this again, okay? We already talked about it. I'm not interested in John Tyler. And even if I was—he's a baby."

Not a chuckle this time, but a hoot of laughter.

"Okay," Ali conceded. "Not a baby."

"A very big boy, in fact," Peg added with an ornery smile.

"That may be. But he's still too young for me."

"Meaning if he wasn't, you might be tempted?"

Exasperated, Ali groaned. "What part of no isn't registering here? *No.* I would *not* be interested. I swear, you're worse than he is when it comes to lost causes. And that's what this is. A certified lost cause."

"If you say so."

"Oh, great. Now I'm getting attitude."

"Only because I think he might be good for you."

"Excuse me? What happened to 'Watch out for that boy, Ali. He's trouble.'"

"Yeah, well, he is…but only if you're looking for something he's not willing to give."

Ali wrinkled her brow. "So you're saying that as long as I'm aware he's only good for a good time, it's okay?" She shook her head. "Sorry. That's not the way I'm wired."

Peg considered her thoughtfully, then sat back down beside her. "Okay, look. For the record, J.T.'s a great guy. I love him like a brother. Even considered something more with him before Cutter and I got together.

"The thing is," she continued, "I know him—well, at least I *used* to know him and what made him tick. But that was before he left Sundown for the West Coast a few years ago. Before he enlisted in the marines. He's been different since then. He goes through women like…oh, I don't know, like he's trying to break a speed record or something, and believe me, he's opted for quantity instead of quality."

She paused, shook her head as if she wished she understood what had happened to change him. "But I know that deep down he's a good man. And even though I've only known you for a month or so, I think I know you, too. You two remind me of each other in some ways. Something's missing for both of you. Something…I don't know, something about both of you fairly shouts that you need more—if you'd let yourselves have it. I just keep thinking that maybe you could find it in each other."

"What I needed I found in David," Ali said, accepting that her friend meant well. Peg was the only soul in Sundown who knew Ali was a widow and she'd sworn her to secrecy. One of the things she'd wanted to get away from when she moved from Kansas City was the widow stigma. She didn't like labels. And she guarded her privacy like a hawk. Always had, which was why it surprised her she'd confided in Peg. "When he died, that need died, too. I can guarantee you I'm not going to find what I had with David in John Tyler. And whatever you think John's missing, he's not going to find it in me, either."

Peg reached out, squeezed her hand. "Okay. But, if you ever change your mind, at the very least, he'd be a real good time. We can all use a stress reliever from time to time, if you get my drift."

Ali could only laugh over Peg's well-intentioned tenacity. "I live for stress. It's what keeps me going.

"Speaking of stress relievers—" She squinted up at Peg. "Go home to yours. I've got work to do. I'd like to get a coat of paint on the living room yet tonight and I don't have time to entertain your X-rated fantasies as they might apply to my life."

"Okay, fine, but if you'd wait until Saturday I could help. Cutter's taking Shelby on a campout and Mom's always looking for an excuse to get her hands on Dawson, so I'll have some time on my hands."

Ali envied Peg her beautiful family. Shelby, her ten-year-old tomboy and little Dawson, the two-year old image of his daddy, were walking testimony to the love Peg and Cutter shared.

"Don't worry," she said, pushing back the regrets that she and David had never gotten around to starting their own family. "If that's how you want to spend your day off, I'll still have plenty to keep you busy. The Realtor was a master of understatement when he told me this house was a fixer-upper.

"Go," she added shooing Peg toward her truck. "Give Shelby and Dawson hugs for me. You can hug Cutter for me, too," Ali added just to show that she appreciated what Peg had waiting for her at home.

"Happy to oblige on all counts." Peg headed down the walk. "See you Saturday, if not before."

Ali painted for a couple of hours after Peg left. Satisfied that she'd put in enough hours for one day and feeling her muscles burn from her tussle with the calf and the paint roller, she took a hot shower, slipped on a sleep shirt then ate a light dinner. It was almost ten o'clock by the time she poured herself a glass of iced tea and headed outside to her back porch to wind down a bit before turning in.

And as she stood there in her bare feet, comfortably aware of the silence of the night, she thought about what Peg had said. Sometimes making more out of less *could* be a good thing. She leaned a shoulder against a porch post badly in need of painting, and hoped that in time her less would become more.

For now though, she wasn't sure. Wasn't sure that her bright idea of living out David's dream was the best way to keep in touch with the memory of the husband she had lost to cancer long before either one of them was ready for him to go. She so wished his dream could have happened for him—that together, they could have moved west, experienced the mountains and the slower pace, played at turning back time and, together, lived a way of life that was as much a part of American history as it was a part of the American present. At least it was in Sundown, Montana.

He'd have loved it here, she realized, blinking back tears.

And thinking about what could've been was ground she had no business treading this time of night. It was late and she was tired and it would be too easy to think herself into a major funk.

On a deep breath, she looked around her and tapped back into some of the other reasons she'd signed on the dotted line—for both the business and this old rattletrap of a house.

She'd needed a change. She'd grown stale and stagnant in Kansas City, mired in memories and the past. One morning two months ago she'd awakened, taken a good look at herself in the mirror and seen little more than the shell of the person she used to be. Talk about being hit by a truck. Right then and there, she'd decided she had to do something or she was going to shrivel up like a dried prune and finally blow away like dust. David wouldn't have wanted that. He would have wanted her to move on with her life.

It had taken her four years, but she'd finally moved on to Montana and a new adventure. And a very old house, she thought with a sigh. Actually, she loved the house…peeling paint, cracked plaster, banged-up hardwood floors and all. In her mind's eye, she tried to picture it as it had once been—a queenly painted Victorian lady, with her gingerbread trim refurbished in rainbow colors and the stained-glass window above the foyer door restored so the hummingbird that was its focal point could spread its wings again and fly.

The mountains, of course, had been another draw and remained a wonder to her. And the air out here was like nothing she'd ever breathed before, pure and crisp and scented of pine and sometimes dust but always free of smog-choked city air. The night sky…the night sky was a stargazer's dream.

"Look at that moon," she murmured aloud just to assure herself she was actually a part of all this wide-open and quiet beauty. It was a lover's moon peeking down tonight. And because that thought made her a little misty for what she no longer had in her life, she decided it was time to turn in before she morphed a beautiful evening into a full-scale pity party.

The phone rang just as she walked back into the kitchen.

"Not tonight," she groaned, anticipating an emergency vet call as the screen door creaked closed behind her. The vets in the county rotated through an on-call schedule and she was the designated doc for the night.

As she picked up, she reached for a note pad and prepared herself mentally to dig deep for another charge to her inner battery. She'd need one heck of a jump-start to make another ranch call tonight.

"Doctor Samuels."

"Hey, Doc. How's it going?"

John Tyler. She'd recognize that rust-and-honey voice anywhere.

Her fingers tightened around her pen while her heart did a clumsy cartwheel. And what did that say, she wondered, about the effect he really had on her?

It said that he annoyed her. *That's* what it said. He just plain annoyed her. Period.

Okay. So she was working it a little hard. It was easy to take that tack with Peg, but when it was just her and her conscience, the "annoys me" argument didn't ring quite as true.

She really didn't understand. She truly wasn't interested in getting involved with him—with anyone for that matter—yet every time he turned his latte-brown eyes and bad-boy grin her way, she felt an edgy awareness hum through her system, keeping pace with the denial. Now, it seemed, all she had to do was hear his voice and things started humming again.

"You still there, Doc?"

She could picture his cocky self on the other end of the line. He was rough and tough, brash and bold as only a true cowboy, one who'd grown up in the life, could be. Sure, there was no denying that he was also wildly gorgeous. He knew it, too, bone deep, like a baby knows one dimple-cheeked and drooling grin could turn the most stoic skeptic into a babbling idiot. Peg had described him as one of those men who oozed confidence and competence—and wore both in a way that made men respect him and women wonder what it would take to tame him.

Well, *some* women at any rate. She just didn't happen to be one of them. At least, she didn't want to be.

"Doc?"

"Yes," she snapped, then immediately regretted it. Irritated with herself for letting him rattle her, she settled herself. "I'm here."

"But I called too late, didn't I?"

His apologetic tone made her feel bad suddenly because she was being so huffy. It wasn't his fault that she didn't like how she reacted to him. Still, this needed to stop. For all his obvious charm, even more obvious were his motives. John Tyler was on the make. It was his M.O. Saw it as his calling, according to Peg, to fill the role of the county's heartbreaker.

"What did you want, John?"

"Oh-oh. It's worse than I thought. I can feel the chill all the way out here. Not only did I call too late, I woke you up, didn't I?"

She sighed, weary of dealing with the entire situation. "You didn't wake me."

"Good. 'Cause the last thing I wanted to do was—"

"John—"

"J.T." he interrupted. "I keep telling you, my friends call me J.T."

"J.T." she repeated pointedly, "do you need a vet?"

"Nope. No vet. Everything's fine. I was just thinking about that shot you took on the chin today and wanted to check on you before I hit the sack…make sure you're all right."

Okay. This she didn't need—affirmation that Peg might be right. That he was a nice guy as well as a Casanova. "My chin is fine. Thanks for asking. So, if there's nothing else you need…"

She trailed off when she heard his low chuckle on the other end of the line, only then realizing what she'd said and done.

If there's nothing else you need…

She'd just opened the door for one of his patented come-ons.

Good going, Ali.

He didn't step through it, though. He didn't have to. His sexy laugh said it all. He knew what she was thinking, just like he knew that she knew he knew and that was enough for him.

She shook her head, drew herself out of her little mental trip back to junior high. "Good night, John—J.T."

"'Night, Doc. You sleep tight, now."

The smile in his voice felt warm and fuzzy with just enough huskiness thrown in to let her know that if she had trouble sleeping, he had the cure for her insomnia.

"Unbelievable," she muttered as she disconnected.

Alone in her kitchen, with the fatigue of the day wearing away at her defenses and no one to run interference, she was forced to face some uncomfortable truths. She didn't want to be, but she was a little too aware of that young cowboy. In person or over the phone line, he was one big testosterone-charged obstacle that kept reminding her he really was a man—not a boy— and that she was still a woman.

Leaning a hip against her kitchen table, she forked her hair back from her face and wondered what in the world she was going to do about him. About this pretty young man who made no bones about what he wanted to happen between them and who, for the first time in four years, made her think about the fact that she'd once had a healthy sex life. That she'd had wants and needs and desires.

And the really hard part? For the first time in four years, he made her think about the fact that even though David had been her soul mate, her one true love, she hadn't died when he had.

J.T. had been thinking—a surefire way to get himself in trouble. At least, that's what his dad always said. The particular kind of trouble he had a mind to stir up this morning had gorgeous blue eyes and lips so sensual and sweet that just thinking about them had prompted him to take more than his fair share of cold showers lately. As distractions went, she was a major player.

So, as he snagged his truck keys and headed out the door Saturday morning, what he was thinking was that it was about time he met Doc Dish on her turf instead of his where she always had her professional face on. And the fact was, he just plain wanted to see that whole pretty package again when she wasn't frowning over a sick calf or a lame colt or a mare with the strangles.

When he pulled up in front of her house and cut the motor, though, he experienced an unfamiliar moment of hesitation. This could be a mistake. The lady had made it plenty clear that she had about as much inclination to become romantically involved with him as a wild horse had a mind to be broken to ride. At least in words and deeds she'd made that clear. Her eyes though, and that sexy little tremor in her voice, sent other signals. There was something going on behind all that denial and it felt a lot more like a yes to him than a no. And he was far too interested to give it up until he'd made a better effort to swing her around to his way of thinking.

Determined to do just that, he loped up her front porch steps and rapped his knuckles on the screen door.

"Come on in. Door's open."

Okay. He could go two ways with this. Clearly, she was expecting someone and it sure as the world wasn't him. He could do the right thing, ID himself and give her a chance to come up with an excuse not to let him in, or he could walk on in and catch her off guard.

Like there was any contest.

With an ornery grin, he stepped through the door. And there she was, standing on a stepladder in the dining room, her back to him, rolling cream-colored paint in the corner where wall met ceiling.

Holy longhorn.

She was dressed for the heat, yet in bare feet, a pair of worn jean short shorts and a skimpy little white tube-type top that left a whole lot of skin bare both above and below it, she looked anything but cool.

What she looked was hot.

Lord have mercy, did she look hot.

He'd never seen her in anything but working jeans and T-shirts and clunky boots but he'd been pretty sure there was a tidy little female form underneath them. Man, oh, man, was there. He hadn't been prepared, though, for the punch of lust that shot through him now that he knew exactly what she'd been covering up. And it took seeing her like this to finally get a handle on why he was so intrigued.

The doc was a mature woman. Complete with a mature woman's body, soft and supple and lush. He liked it. He liked that while her legs were short and slender and her calves were strong and firm, there was a soft resilience about her thighs and hips. He liked very much that there was a gentle roundness to her bottom that a man could just sink his hands into. Some women her age might fret and stew over the fact that their body wasn't as toned and firm as it had once been. Some might worry over every little wrinkle on their face. He had a strong gut feeling that the doc wouldn't give much thought to, either. She was comfortable with who she was and how she looked. Confident. He thought it was sexy as hell.

And the truth was, he'd had his fill of calendar girls. Pretty young things with smooth, flawless skin and firm toned muscles—and often nothing much going on inside except concern over how their hair looked, was their lipstick smeared and did the pants they were wearing make their butt look big.

The doc was different…not just outside, but in, and that was part and parcel of why he was taking a chance coming here today. Nothing he'd seen so far made him think he'd made a mistake.

She'd pulled her hair up on top of her head in a no-frills topknot. And while most of it stayed put, the silky strands that had escaped tumbled down her back in wispy wheat-gold ribbons to tickle her bare shoulders when she stretched to reach a spot in the corner. It also gave him a little extra glimpse of skin when she lifted her arms above her head and her shorts rode a little lower on her hips.

She had the most amazing skin…not pale as he'd imagined it, but sort of a light, golden tan that looked silky smooth and so touchable his hands had started to itch with the need to find out just how it felt up close and personal.

Up close and personal, however, was the very least he wanted to be with this woman.

That's when he decided. It was a done deal. He and the reluctant Alison Samuels were going to become real good friends. *Real good.* And wearing her down was going to be half the fun.

"You sure you're up for this?" she asked without turning around. "Not exactly a great way to spend your day off."

He thumbed back his hat, shoved his fingertips into the front pockets of his jeans and leaned a shoulder against the doorjamb. "Oh, I don't know…it's looking pretty good from where I'm standing."

Three

Ali froze. The amused, sexy drawl was about two octaves lower than Peg's. John Tyler's voice also had an effect on her that Peg's never would—and right now, it was making her pulse spike and launching a fleet of butterflies into liftoff in her tummy.

When she slowly turned and saw the smug smile tilting his generous, flirty lips, she became painfully aware of what she was wearing and that the cowboy had been getting an eyeful.

"Hello," he said, all little-boy eyes and impish grin.

With a very deliberate movement, calculated to assure herself as much as him that she had things under control, she lowered the roller onto the paint tray. "I was expecting Peg."

"Life's just full of little surprises, huh?"

The air was close and hot. She was already tired. And she just wasn't up to sparring with the likes of John Tyler. "Isn't it just?"

"Got yourself a major project going here, I see. Need any help?"

She forced herself to smile down at him. Friendly and polite. Approachable yet distant. Woman to *boy*. "The Titanic needed help. I need a miracle."

And she needed to get off this ladder because judging by the look on his face, he was having a little too much fun enjoying the view.

Trying to ignore how rattled his company made her, she took a backward step down and, "Ohmygod!" completely missed the ladder rung. She felt herself falling, was aware of her arms flailing in open air and braced for the impact.

"Hey, hey." A pair of strong arms scooped her up and lifted her up against his chest. "Whoa, now. That was quite a dismount. Not to mention a great way to break your neck."

Breathless, her heart hammering, Ali blinked up into his startled but smiling eyes and couldn't think of a single thing to say. Or do. Only one thing was certain. She didn't dare move. Not with him holding her like a groom carrying his bride across the threshold. Not with his fingers pressing against the side of her breast and a sudden awareness that her bandeau top had slipped so far south that even breathing represented a huge risk. In fact, she had a sneaking suspicion that if she made one wrong move, she'd give a whole new meaning to overexposure.

Wasn't this special?

Even more special was the adrenaline rush. It hit her like a ball bat and, for all intents and purposes, paralyzed her. For the life of her, all she could do was lie there in his arms, hyperaware of the heat of his body against hers—specifically his warm fingers digging into the soft swell of breast tissue under her arm. No one had touched her there since…well, no one had touched her there in a very, very long time. The fact that she was being touched there now awakened reflexes and re-sponse triggers that had lain dormant for years.

Without warning, her nipples tightened as blood flooded them to aching sensitivity. And for one insane, intense and sexually charged moment, her mind's eye flashed on the image of John Tyler's dark head bent over her breast, of his generous, mobile lips caressing her nipple, his tongue laving it as his mouth alternately kissed and…

"Hey…hey. Doc? Sweetie, you're shaking like a leaf. You okay?" His voice broke into her thoughts, penetrat-ing the sound of blood rushing through her ears.

No. No, she was not okay. She was mortified. And aroused and…and confused.

"I, um…I'm fine. I…a…delayed reaction to the fall, I guess. I…I don't know how I could have been so clumsy."

"Might have been the line about the Titanic," he said

easily. "The mention of one disaster courted another. Although, as disasters go, I've got to say, I like the way this one played out."

Yeah. She just bet he did. A quick check confirmed that she was still covered—barely—but resurrected the unsettling visual image of his mouth making love to her breast.

Talk about a dangerous fall. She needed to snap out of it—no easy feat when she was swamped with an acute awareness of the strength of the arms that held her, of the breadth of the chest beneath his white T-shirt, of his heart beating steady and true and picking up speed where it pressed against her.

How could she have forgotten all the wonderful differences in the physique of a woman and a man? How could she have forgotten this wonderful sensation of being a woman, pressed against a man?

By blocking it from her mind, that's how. When the nights had become so long and cold and empty because she'd missed David so much, forgetting had been the only way to survive.

On a bracing breath, she calmed herself and finally felt the blood return to her brain where it belonged. Along with it, the feeling returned to her arms—and just in the nick of time. She lifted a hand and made what she hoped was a discreet adjustment on her top.

"You can put me down now," she said, her voice whisper-soft as she looked up and into a pair of eyes so dark brown they were almost black.

She meant to look away. Really, she did. But at this close range, his eyes were as fascinating as they were beautiful. She could see the full range of browns in his irises—cinnamon, chocolate, earth. All intense, all warm, like his lashes which were sable-dark and silky thick. Years of smiling and hours in the sun had dug creases at the corners that added to rather than detracted from eyes that held far too much sway over her reactions when she absolutely did not want to think about him in any way other than as a client and acquaintance.

A tough trick when so much of her was in direct contact with so much of him. The heat and the dizzying scent of him didn't help, either: sage and a little sweat and, woven through it, the scent of leather.

"John?"

"J.T." he insisted, holding her gaze with a little too much heat.

"J.T…I said, you can put me down now."

"I could, you're right, but the question is, are you steady enough? I mean, I'd hate to see you try for another header into the floor. How about we don't take that chance and I just hold on for a little while yet?"

She narrowed her eyes. "How about we live dangerously?"

He grinned but slowly lowered her to her feet. "Can't blame a guy for trying. Besides, it's not often an opportunity like this falls into my arms."

Once she was on her feet and able to put a little distance between them, her emotional as well as her physical equilibrium returned. She wasn't sure what had just happened to her but she knew it was an anomaly. She was not getting involved with him. In the first place, she didn't want to; in the second, it was ludicrous. It had nothing to do with running away from her feelings. She wasn't running. She wasn't scared, even though the feelings rustling around inside her walked like, talked like and overall made a pretty convincing imitation of fear.

So she experienced a little case of happy hormones when she was around him. She didn't have to act on them. Before this got any further out of hand, though, she needed to make him understand that a boat with him and her in it just wasn't going to float.

But how? Resistance hadn't worked. Maybe she simply needed to convince him that he didn't get to her...which meant she needed to treat him like she would any other man who did not heat her blood and make her question, why, exactly, the idea of a friendly affair with him was such a bad idea.

"Guess it's a good thing for me you showed up. The last thing I need is a sprained anything."

"My pleasure. Promise me you'll be more careful from now on."

"Lesson learned," she said. "The practice is too busy and I've got too much work to do on the house to put myself out of commission."

"Well," he said, with a long, lingering sweep of his gaze down the length of her body that had her fingers itching to tug on her top again even though she was all tucked in, "things really are shaping up nicely."

An involuntary shiver ripped from her breast to her belly and back again at the blatant heat in his eyes that made it very clear he wasn't just talking about the house.

All right. This must stop. Right now. As angry at herself for letting him draw these reactions out of her as she was at him for prompting them, she squared her shoulders, primed to deliver a very clear message.

"John—"

"You know," he said before she got any further, "I can still remember when this house used to be the town showplace."

His statement stopped her cold.

"You can? Really? You remember how she looked in her prime?" She'd been desperate to know more about the house but hadn't had time to search for pictures. "I want very badly to restore her to her original colors and style."

"Her?"

"Absolutely." She averted her eyes from his amused grin and bent to pick up a paint rag to wipe her hands. "She's every inch a lady."

"And you know this because…?"

She lifted a shoulder. "It's just a feeling. There's an underlying softness about her…in the graceful curve of the woodwork, the spindled banister…even in the leaded glass windows." She let her gaze drift around the room. "Yes. The house is definitely a beautiful, elegant lady."

"Just like her owner," he said and had her heart going all fluttery again.

And again, she felt self-disgust for reacting. She worked at wiping the bulk of the paint from her fingers. *Studied* her fingers, actually, so she wouldn't be compelled to study him. Or to be taken in again by those sexy brown eyes and by the way he looked in his chest-hugging white T-shirt, tight, worn jeans and gray cowboy hat—like he'd been the man the entire cowboy look had been created for.

"I don't remember the kind of details you're wanting," he said, making her realize she'd been staring. Fortunately he was inspecting the woodwork around a pair of pocket doors separating the foyer from the dining room, and hadn't noticed. "But I might be able to find them for you."

"You're kidding. How?"

"My mom was president of the Gray County Historical Society until Dad retired and they moved to California. She's no longer active with the organization but I'll bet she has some old photographs of this place. And even if she doesn't, she'd know where to find them. I'll give her a call. See if I can turn something up."

"That would be wonderful," she said, caught up in the excitement of the possibility of finding some significant information on the house. "I mean, if it's not too much trouble."

"No trouble. Plus I'll get mega brownie points for not only calling her but showing an interest in one of her pet projects."

Ali had to smile in spite of herself. "And what do these points net you?"

"Oh, it's big. Real big. She'll send a box of home-made fudge for sure." His grin was guileless and, she thought with reluctance, endearing. "Probably a box of cookies. Oatmeal-raisin are my favorite, by the way… just in case I'm making points with you, too."

Okay. So he was annoying. He was also charming. And sexy. And he'd just dangled a very delectable carrot. She wanted those photos. "Show me results and I might be persuaded to show you some cookies."

He grinned again, slow and sexy, his thoughts as clear as the Montana sky. No doubt he'd like her to show him her cookies, all right, and a whole lot more.

"In the meantime," she said, giving up on lecturing him—he was incorrigible, anyway—she led the way to the kitchen, "you want to tell me why you stopped by? And don't say to ask me out to dinner because we've already established that's not going to happen."

There. That was good. Decisive. To the point. See? She could do this. She could keep it neat and tidy and benign. She was being neighborly. And feeling a little self-conscious again, suddenly—not about whether or not she was going to pop out of her top but about what he thought of the way she looked in it.

Figure that one out. Sheer female vanity, she supposed, something she wasn't used to experiencing. She was carrying about five too many pounds and ten too many years to pull off short shorts and a tube top—although it hadn't seemed to be any effort at all for him to catch her and hold her in his arms. She didn't care if Peg saw her this way but she'd never intended for anyone else to see her like this.

Maybe it was a good thing that John had. Maybe he'd realize there was nothing subtle about the differences between a thirty-year-old and a forty-year-old woman's body and he'd cool his jets. She kept in shape, she took care of herself and she was good with the way she looked, but Mother Nature and gravity were power players. Like City Hall, you could fight them but you'd never win.

If she'd been into masochism, she'd make sure he got a good, long look. But thinking about long looks started her thinking about the close call with her top so in the end she snagged the T-shirt she'd thrown over a kitchen chair earlier and tugged it over her head.

Walking to the fridge, she pulled out a pitcher of tea. And because it would be just plain rude not to, she offered him a glass when she poured one for herself.

He shook his head. "Thanks, but I never did get a taste for the stuff. Water'd be great though. And since you said not to tell you that I came to ask you out to dinner, I won't. How about we go dancing instead?"

So much for cooling his jets.

"Don't dance," she countered, plopped some ice cubes in a glass of water and held it out to him.

While she couldn't prove it, it seemed that he very deliberately touched her fingers with his as she pulled her hand away. Once again, she had to divorce herself from the sensations his touch stirred to life and the reminder of how rough and steady he'd felt holding her. She'd sensed a restrained strength that came from years of working cattle and made her wonder if he was rough or gentle with a woman—and which she would want him to be with her.

Do not *go there.*

"I suppose you don't watch movies, either."

Feeling her face flush from her wayward thoughts, she shook her head. No way was she even going to think about sitting beside him in a dark theater, their fingers colliding in the middle of a bag of buttered popcorn. "No time. Between the practice and this house, I'm pretty well tied up."

She could feel his gaze on her, watching her over the lip of his glass, and had to fight an unexpected urge to reach up and tuck stray strands of hair back into her topknot. She'd caught a glimpse of her reflection in the window above the kitchen sink. Her hair was a mess. Complete with a couple streaks of paint. She wasn't wearing a speck of makeup. Not even lipstick.

And why should she, she thought in self-disgust. She was working here. She wasn't out to impress anyone. Especially John Tyler.

He, however, seemed determined to impress her.

"So, I can't take you to dinner or dancing or to a movie. Guess I'll have to offer my services in some other capacity. How's the wiring?"

Oh, no. That's exactly what she didn't need—a young superstud cowboy sauntering through her house looking capable and male and helpful. Even more, she didn't need him in her house *being* capable and male and helpful. She was an independent woman, but one of the things she missed most about being half of a couple was that inherent skill a man seemed to be born with for fixing things. The way a man looked when he was taking care of things for a woman.

"I couldn't possibly ask you to do that."

"You didn't ask. I offered."

"Well, I can't accept."

He slanted her an amused look. "What? There's a law or something?"

"Of course not. It just wouldn't be right. You've got plenty of your own work to do without investing time in mine. How's that calf, by the way?" she added quickly, determined to get him off the subject so he'd get the message that she did not want him here.

"He's getting along. And I think I can decide whether I've got time to spare or not. Now, about that wiring…"

Ali wasn't sure how he managed it, but somehow the persistent Mr. Tyler ended up staying through the morning, working alongside her until Peg arrived a little while later. Then she and Peg painted and he ran up and down stairs in his cowboy boots, T-shirt and jeans, into the attic, down to the basement and back to the main floor again checking out her wiring. By noon, she'd worked up a sweat just watching him. So, evidently, had he, because his T-shirt came off a little while later.

Peg, ornery soul that she was, made sure to point it out, then give Ali an earful about what a "hottie" he was.

"Hottie?" Ali snorted. "Sweetie, you've got to graduate from teen magazines."

Peg just chuckled. "Look, I know centerfold material when I see it. That man has abs to die for."

"Does Cutter know you drool over other men like this?"

"I'm not drooling, hon. I'm merely observing. You're the one who's drooling."

"Am not."

"Are, too."

When Peg snickered, Ali threw down her paint roller in disgust—mostly because she *might* have been drooling. A little. And reliving that disturbing fantasy of his mouth on her breast.

She was pathetic. And not thinking with her head. Maybe it was the heat.

"Know what I think?" Peg used a thin brush to trim next to the woodwork.

"Would it matter if I said I don't care what you think?"

"I think," Peg went on, oblivious to Ali's sarcasm, "that you're lying to yourself where J.T. is concerned. I think," she continued, way too smug to suit Ali, "that you ought to listen to your heart."

"Believe me. My heart has nothing to do with this."

But her libido did, she finally admitted and couldn't

stop herself from taking a peek when John walked by the door, a roll of electrical wire slung over his shoulder. His bare shoulder. That was muscled and tan. Like his chest and arms.

Had a man *ever* looked that good in jeans?

Oh Lord. She'd lost complete control. When had that happened?

And when had it gotten so late, she wondered later. More to the point, why did she smell pizza?

"Dusk to Dawn special," John said, carrying a large pizza box into the house. "Don't know about you two, but I'm starved."

He plopped the pizza down on the floor in the middle of the protective paint tarp and opened the brown paper bag that sat on top of the box. "Bread sticks. And soda."

"I thought you went to the hardware store," Ali said.

He dug a small bag full of nails out of his hip pocket and held them up so she could see that he had, indeed, stopped at the hardware store.

"Wow. I didn't realize it had gotten so late." Peg stood abruptly. "I've got to go pick up the baby and head for home."

"What? You're leaving?" Ali scrambled after her when she headed for the door, panicked by the prospect of being alone with John. It was becoming almost impossible to keep thinking of John as the young boy she kept saying he was. "You can't leave," she insisted with an imploring look.

"What, you didn't work me hard enough today?" Peg teased, deliberately ignoring Ali's plea.

"No. I mean yes. Yes, I worked you hard. But…you need to eat something before you go."

"I'll eat at home. Cutter and Shelby promised to bring fish home from their camp-out. I'll be expected to eat it."

With a cheery goodbye, she headed out, leaving Ali exactly where she didn't want to be. Alone with a man who'd been trying to get her alone for the better part of a month.

"Well," John said, innocent as the proverbial babe. "Guess we're having dinner together after all. Funny how that worked out."

"Yeah. Funny."

This cowboy was calculating and evil. And gorgeous. And too clever for his own good.

And thoughtful, she conceded, eying the box of pizza. Urgh.

If she refused to share it, she'd look ungrateful and bitchy. He'd worked like a dog all day—on *her* house, regardless that she hadn't asked him to. Yet he'd clearly known what he was doing and he'd saved her money and time.

The least she could be was gracious.

"I'm paying for dinner," she said in a no-nonsense tone that invited no arguments.

Evidently he decided he'd pushed her as far as he dared because he didn't argue when she fished a twenty out of her wallet and handed it to him cover the cost of the pizza.

"Okay. I'll let you have your way…this time." He reluctantly pocketed the bill. "But next time, dinner's on me."

There wasn't going to be a next time, she assured herself. Somehow, some way, she was going to nip this in the bud.

"Yeah. I like it," John said in response to Ali's question about whether or not he liked ranching.

She'd decided that he was a safe topic while they munched on pizza and sipped soda in the middle of her dining room floor. He was all covered up with his T-shirt again—and she'd made sure she stayed covered up. Thankfully, the barrier of the added clothes seemed to be an effective deterrent because he'd backed off on his flirting. Either that or he was really tired. He'd already told her about his two sisters, one married and living in California, the other at NYU completing her masters in child development.

"Took a while to get to that point though," he continued. "I was like most kids growing up, I guess. When all you know is the ranch, all you want to know is the fastest way away from it."

He reached into the box for another slice of pizza. Ali couldn't make herself look away from the ripple effect that small movement had on his entire body. Okay, so his clothes didn't entirely stop her from thinking about what he looked like underneath them.

He was stretched out on his side, his weight on one

elbow, one leg cocked, his knee swinging lazily back and forth as he alternately ate and talked. As relaxed as he was, there was no mistaking the strength and condition of the muscle and sinew beneath his T-shirt and jeans. His forearms fascinated her. The way the veins running beneath his skin stood out like ropy rivers, like the muscle beneath forced them toward the surface, drew her attention again and again.

David had had a runner's body, lean and long but with few of the fascinating bulges and contours this rancher wore and that told of the hard physical work he did on a daily basis.

"What changed your mind?" she asked, appalled to realize she'd just made a comparison between him and David. Heart beating hard in confusion and guilt, she had to concentrate to tune in to what John was saying.

"A lot of things. After I graduated I commuted to Bozeman and the community college. It was enough of a taste of the city that I wanted more, so I transferred to Colorado State. And to answer your next question, my degree is in computer science."

That bit of information grabbed her undivided attention. "Really?" She'd never figured him for a tech head and he certainly didn't fit the stereotypical nerd profile.

"Yup. Even own a pocket protector to prove it."

He grinned and she couldn't help but do the same.

"Did you ever use your degree?"

"In Sacramento, with a company developing computer games. Made good money, too, creating games so

armchair warriors could play war and annihilate termi-
nator terrorist types."

He sobered abruptly. For a long moment, he simply
stared into space. The room became eerily quiet until
he seemed to realize he'd tuned out on her.

"But you gave it up," she ventured, offering him an
opportunity to pick up on the thread of his conversation.

He nodded, then drew a deep breath, as if he had to
work to compose himself.

"Why?"

He looked at her, his eyes questioning.

"Why did you give it up?"

Another long silence. Another deep breath. "Because
9/11 happened. And suddenly war games didn't seem
like such a great way to be making a living anymore."

Four

The room hummed with a silence that relayed Ali's understanding and John's regret.

"I lost a friend in the attack," he said after a long moment. "While I'd been making games out of war."

"I'm sorry," she said softly, moved but not wanting to be by this new side of him. A thoughtful, troubled side that made her realize he wasn't as one-dimensional as she'd wanted him to be—or as he'd like people to think he was. In fact she was beginning to think he was a very complex man. What he said next confirmed it.

"It's an understatement to say that day changed my life. I did a lot of reassessing after that, you know? Didn't much like what I saw…didn't like that I felt what I was doing didn't make much of a difference."

He shrugged, glanced at her then away. "So I took my vacation and flew to NYC. Volunteered for everything and anything. At the end of two weeks…well, let's just say I realized I'd taken our way of life for granted—our freedoms, our security. And I knew I wanted to do more."

She watched his face, watched it harden, watched his eyes, sensing that he wasn't talking to her as much as he was rehashing some decisions that had been life-altering.

"I gave my two weeks notice, walked into the nearest army recruiters office and enlisted. Patriotic duty and all that," he added, his tone discounting that it really had been a patriotic and selfless act. Not to mention dangerous.

"And after my stint with Uncle Sam, I knew what I wanted to do and where I wanted to be. Back here in Sundown."

She didn't have to be a mind reader to understand that there was more, much more to the story than that. His eyes had grown vacant and dark when he'd mentioned his military service. *Army.* They'd seen—continued to see—a lot of action in the war on terror. Peg said he wasn't the same person when he'd come back to Sundown.

Ali couldn't help but wonder if he'd been in the thick of it, but sensed she'd be doing them both a favor if she didn't ask. If he wanted to talk about it he would. And she really didn't want to know. At least that's what she told herself. She didn't *need* to know any more about him.

Knowledge, in this instance, wasn't power. Knowledge—specifically about him—was weakening her position. The more she found out, the more she wanted to know.

She was beginning to like him, was more than a little intrigued by him, by what had happened in his past that had, for the briefest of moments, made his eyes go dark with pain. And no matter how desperately she didn't want to own up to it, this attraction she felt for him was a little too strong.

It was…troubling. David had been her one and only. She'd never, in the past four years without him, seen herself with another man. Not as a lover. Not as a partner. Not in any capacity. So, it was unsettling, this effect John had on her.

Unsettling but under control, she assured herself.

"What about you?" he asked into a silence that had started to get uncomfortably long.

The fan she'd set in the open window drew in a pleasant stirring of dew-damp air from outside, cooling the room.

"Me? Not much to tell."

"Humor me."

The lighthearted flirt was back. Just like that. Like he'd flipped a switch.

"Okay…well, I had Ward and June Cleaver for parents, grew up in the 'burbs of Chicago and have two brothers I adore."

"Nice, neat storybook life, huh?"

For a while, yes. Definitely a storybook life.

"Yes," she agreed with a tight smile. "It pretty much was."

He didn't say anything when she didn't elaborate but she could feel his gaze sharpen on her face as she shifted position, crossing her legs in front of her. She propped her elbows on her knees and dangled her soda between them.

"Bet you were a cheerleader," he said with a speculative look.

That prompted a laugh. "Not quite…although one of my best friends was. I was the class brain."

"Ah. Now there's a heavy burden to bear." A dimpled grin undercut his sympathy.

"One of my own making. All I did was study. Wanted to be the best, you know. Missed a lot of things I sometimes regret—dances, parties—but it paid off when I applied for college and then vet school."

"Which brings me to a question that's been bugging me. Why?"

"Why am I a vet? Because I love animals. And I love science and medicine."

He shook his head. "No…I mean, why here?"

"You mean as opposed to some cushy small-animal clinic where the big bucks and easy money is made?"

"Exactly."

She shrugged then hedged a bit. "I needed a change. Wanted to experience another aspect of the practice. And I've always had a thing for the mountain west."

It wasn't a lie, exactly. It just wasn't the whole truth. He didn't need to know that it had been David's dream to come here. Didn't need to know it was David's dream she was trying to make come true. In fact, he didn't need to know about David at all.

She was very confused about the physical reaction she'd had to John earlier. In retrospect, it felt very much like she'd betrayed David. Now, to talk about David to the man who had initiated that betrayal, well, it would be one more thing to feel ashamed about.

"Still," John added, bringing her back to their conversation, "there are small-animal practices in a hundred little towns around here."

She nodded. "I know. And I considered it. Honestly, I almost went that route…then the Realtor showed me Dr. Sebring's listing and it opened up such a broad spectrum of possibilities."

"Back aches, long hours…bruised chins," he added with a hitch of his chin.

She smiled. Despite all the conflicting emotions darting around inside her, she'd relaxed a little around him. "This is true and maybe if I'd known then what I know now I would have passed. Believe me, there are days when I think I should have, but in that moment, it was like the proverbial dream scene played out in my head. Horses, mountains, small town…and I made the decision on the spot to buy it."

"Just like that."

She took a sip of her soda. "Just like that. So here I am."

"All by yourself," he added, clearly fishing for more information about her personal life.

She didn't intend to fill him in. "All by myself."

"So, there's no one pining away for you back in K.C? No Mr. Right?"

"No," she said, heard the pain in that one small word and forced a smile. "Just my parents. They weren't too pleased about me leaving. They helped me move, though, and once they saw Sundown they were pretty much satisfied I'd be back home by the end of the first week so that cheered them up."

He chuckled. "I imagine it's pretty alien to a city dweller."

"Good choice of words. As far as they're concerned, I landed on a different planet."

"Well, welcome to Mars, Doc." He lifted his can of soda in toast. "K.C.'s loss is definitely Sundown's gain."

She had little choice but to touch her own soda to his. "We can hope. I'm still learning the lay of the land...still struggling with the change to large animal practice, but I enjoy the challenge."

"A challenge is definitely something I can appreciate and relate to," he said, the look in his eyes intensifying as he watched her. "And like you, I always figure on winning."

It was a loaded statement if she'd ever heard one and because it was, she ignored it. "Right now, my main goal is keeping my head above water. I knew it would be busy but never dreamed there'd be so much travel. That should settle down a bit by next week. Dayton clinic's new vet is coming on board and he'll fill a huge hole in the rotation schedule."

"Between work and the house, you're going to wear yourself out."

She shrugged. "I like to keep busy."

"To the exclusion of a social life?"

"Social life? In Sundown? Isn't that a bit of an oxymoron?"

"Good point," he agreed with a quick flash of beautiful white teeth, "although you'd be surprised in the ways we find to have fun around here. I was thinking more about when you were in Kansas City."

"I had a social life," she said.

"So…you dated?"

It was another fishing expedition and she wasn't going to take the bait.

He must have read the warning look in her eyes because he was quick to clarify. "All I was going to say was that I can't believe a woman like you didn't have a string of men falling in line to go out with you."

"No string. No line," she assured him.

"Amazing. Are all the men in K.C. crazy? Blind? Gay?"

His persistence made her laugh. So did his flattery. But no matter that she'd started to like him a little, no matter that she was unexpectedly attracted to him, she really could not let this get out of hand. "John—J.T.," she amended when he slanted her a pointed look, "you are a really nice guy…"

"Oh, boy. Here comes the big *but*. That's my cue to leave before I get shot down again."

"This isn't a question of shooting you down."

"So how come I feel like I've got a hole in my heart the size of Montana?"

She shook her head at his pained and completely staged expression. "Don't you ever stop?"

"Stop? I'll let you in on a little secret. I haven't even started yet."

When he winked, she groaned. Which made him laugh.

"You're tired," he said, standing abruptly—an effective end to any discussion she might want to launch about why he should just forget about any scenario with him and her as the focal point.

"Get some rest, okay?" He settled his Resistol on his head. "And think 'bout that social life you don't have."

Then he said his good-nights and headed out the door before she'd barely had a chance to thank him for the work he'd done.

Well, she thought, watching his taillights disappear into the night. So much for nipping it in the bud.

And so much for thinking she was dead inside.

As unsettling as it was, from the moment she'd looked down from the ladder and seen him standing there, she'd felt very much alive. Lying alone in bed later that night with no one and nothing running interference, she admitted that when John had held her in his arms and she'd felt all the sinewy male strength wrapped around her…well…it had been incredibly arousing.

A tear trickled down her temple as she lay on her back and stared at the ceiling fighting it, but aching for the touch of a man.

Aching for David, who was gone.

For the first time in a very long time, she cried herself to sleep. Missing her husband. Missing the love they'd shared. And feeling a fear that shook her to her very core. A fear that warned her she might be forgetting little things, important things that she'd wanted to hold onto forever.

Things like how it had felt to be kissed by her husband. Things like the intricate and beautiful color of his eyes when he'd made love to her.

When she finally slept, she dreamed. Of David in the far, far distance. Of John…so close and real and vital. Of herself, weeping over the two pieces of her heart that she held, beating and vulnerable, in the open palms of her hands.

"You people sure know how to throw a party." Ali leaned into Peg, shouting to be heard above the steel guitar, a fast fiddle and the wail of the lead singer putting his all into a Toby Keith drinking song.

"Great band, huh?" Peg yelled back and shoved a glass of draft beer into Ali's hand.

The crowd gathered Saturday night for her official "Welcome to Sundown" party at the Dusk to Dawn sure seemed to think so. The dance floor was packed—so was the bar and all the tables that were filled with dwindling amounts of snacks and empty glasses. Colorful helium-filled welcome balloons swayed on equally colorful ribbons; a huge banner proclaiming WELCOME DR. SAMUELS in rainbow colors hung over the bar.

"Would you just look at her," Peg said, beaming at Shelby as she danced with her daddy, her red boots flying across the floor.

"She's having a good time."

Everyone was. Or at least they seemed to be. Ali had balked at first when Peg had told her the Sundown Chamber of Commerce, led by Peg's friend Crystal Perkins, was planning this welcome get-together in her honor. She just wasn't into parties. Hadn't been for quite some time.

But maybe she'd been taking life too seriously for too long. And as she stood in the midst of this laughing crowd, she was glad she'd agreed to let them go ahead with their plans. It was good for them. And it was proving to be good for her.

She'd met more people in the past couple of hours than she could have met in a year. Everyone in Sundown, as well as everyone within a hundred-mile radius, turned out for a party, it seemed. Many of them had said they'd be bringing their business her way.

Yeah, she thought, telling herself she wasn't searching for the one someone who hadn't shown up. Everyone had made the party but John Tyler.

She told herself she felt relieved, not let down, over his absence. It made things a lot easier on her tonight.

She didn't want to have to deal with his outrageous flirting.

And yet…this was so hard to admit…she felt a little disappointed that he wasn't here. Figure that one out. Maybe the reason she was feeling disappointment was rooted in plain old-fashioned vanity. It had been a long time since a man had looked at her the way John did. And even though she'd known nothing was going to happen between them, his interest had been a bit of an ego boost. To think she still had what it took to attract not only a man, but a younger man at that… Well, it was a surprise, was all. A nice one. And there was nothing wrong in that line of thinking—as long as she recognized it for what it was.

And that little side trip she'd taken into hormoneville—well, it just proved she was human, that was all.

"Hey there, Doctor Dish." Sam Perkins, Crystal's husband—a big, perpetually grinning bear of a man—wrapped a burly arm around her shoulders. "How's it goin'? You havin' a good time?"

"Doctor *Dish?*" Ali repeated, gaping in disbelief. "Is that what you called me?"

"Honey, it's what all the guys call you," Sam said easily, his face cast in half shadow below the brim of his tan hat. "Dr. Sebring was a great vet, but he didn't fill out a pair of jeans like you do. No disrespect meant."

"None taken," Peg chimed in on Ali's behalf. "Ali knows you're all a bunch of clod-kicking yokels who don't know any better than to judge a woman by the way she looks over the way she performs her job. She's just too polite to say it."

"I think I've just been insulted," Sam said, his grin never fading over Peg's good-natured ribbing. "So… Doc. Wanna dance?"

Laughing, Ali shook her head. "Thanks, but I don't dance."

"Well that's about to change, darlin'."

"Strut your stuff, Ali," Peg said with a laugh. "Show 'em what you got."

"I've got *nothing*," Ali called over her shoulder, panic mixed with amusement as Sam swept her out onto the dance floor. These people were fun. Warm, caring and outrageous fun.

Tonight, for the first night since she'd driven into town, green to the gills about the world of the wild Montana west and wondering ever since if this had been the right thing to do, the right place to be, she felt the first faint stirrings of belonging.

John hunkered down on a bar stool in a dark corner and nursed his beer, trying not to be too obvious over his fascination with the guest of honor. But…hell. He *was* fascinated. Part of it was because she really didn't dance, he thought, unable to stall a grin. It was so cute. She didn't have a lick of rhythm and to say she had two left feet was like saying his herd bull had balls.

Unbelievable. He hadn't known women came that way. She could…not…dance. And he ought to know.

Since he'd slipped into the party half an hour ago, he hadn't been able to take his eyes off the good doctor.

Her lack of expertise on the dance floor, however, was just for starters in the fascination department. She hadn't gotten any uglier since he'd seen her last week, that's for sure. He'd kind of been hoping she would. Or that when he saw her again he'd discover that he'd been remembering big. Realize that she wasn't nearly as pretty as his mind had set her up to be or that he wasn't nearly as attracted to her as he'd originally thought. And seeing her again would not only prove it, but might get her out of his system because she just kept insisting that she wasn't interested.

There was just one little problem with that. He *was* interested. Interested enough that he'd told her more about himself than he'd intended the other night at her house. He was still trying to figure it out. Oh, it wasn't that he'd spilled his guts about Afghanistan. That wasn't ever going to happen. It was just…well, he'd talked a lot and it had surprised him, was all.

Surprised him that he hadn't minded talking to her about himself as much as he'd thought he would. Might have told her more if he hadn't realized what a motor-mouth he'd become and put a plug in it.

She, on the other hand, had been pretty tight-lipped about herself.

Still, as often as she said no to the idea of them getting together, there were too many other indicators that said she wanted to say yes—she just didn't want to admit it. As far as he was concerned, figuring out a way to get her to come to terms with that interest made things more interesting.

For the moment, he was content to drink his beer and watch her. She was knockout gorgeous in a soft flowing skirt that swung around the tops of a brand-new pair of butterscotch-colored boots when she moved, and a pale yellow top that left her shoulders and arms bare. She'd worn her hair down—it was the first time he'd seen it that way. And he liked it. Hadn't realized it was so long. The fine blond mass of it trailed midway down her back, turned under at the ends in a soft upside-down question mark of a curl.

It wasn't that her clothes were all that sexy, either. She could have been turned out for church. It sure as the world wasn't church that he thought about, watching her though. Oh, he thought about going down on his knees for this woman, but it wasn't to pray.

When she threw back her head and laughed at something Virgil Watson whispered in her ear, he just plain stopped thinking. She'd never laughed that way for him. And that just didn't set well. It didn't set well at all.

Gaze locked on her, he drained the last of his beer, walked across the dance floor and tapped the man lucky enough to be holding her in his arms on the shoulder.

"I'll be cutting in now," he said, trying to get a read on the doc's face when she realized it was him.

"Well, hell, J.T.," Virgil sputtered, a sour frown turning his mouth into an inverted U. "We was just getting started."

"I'll be cutting in," John repeated, never taking his eyes off Alison's face.

He was peripherally aware of the brash cowhand sputtering as he sauntered away toward the bar. He was hyperaware of the color of her eyes. Russian sage, he thought again, as he'd thought he first time he'd seen them. Silver-blue with shades of gray. And right now, they were watchful and surprised and just a little bit nervous. The good kind of nervous. The kind that said she was glad to see him but didn't want to be.

"Hey, Doc," he said, flashing his warmest smile.

She smiled, too, kind of tight and uncertain. "Hi."

And then they just stood in the middle of the dance floor while all around them couples moved to the music of a lively Brooks and Dunn song.

"Umm," she finally said, "Did you want to dance?"

"With you?" He grinned, shook his head. "No ma'am. You are, for a fact, the worst dancer I've ever seen."

Her eyes widened in shocked surprise and then she laughed, as he'd hoped she would, and the tension dissolved like an ice cube in boiling water. "Then why did you cut in?"

"Because it was just too painful to watch any longer. Come on," he said, taking her hand and leading her toward the back door, "there's something I want to show you."

"Oh John, I don't know. I shouldn't leave. The party's for me after all."

"It's okay. It'll only take a minute. We're just stepping outside. I'll have you back before you're ever missed."

"Okay, what?" she asked a little breathlessly after he'd led her outside through the back door. "What, exactly, did you want to show me?"

"The sky," he said, lifting a hand.

"The sky? Yes. Well." She looked up, looked at him. "There it is, all right. Complete with a moon and stars."

"And way too good to waste."

He watched her eyes as he turned her toward him. Watched the way the moonlight played across her face as he pulled her into his arms. Watched her expression transition from surprise to wariness to—thank God above—anticipation.

"John."

Even though he kept trying to get her to call him J.T., he loved how she said his name. Loved the little tremor in her voice, the breathlessness. And instead of heeding the slow shake of her head, he played to the anticipation instead and wrapped her tighter against him.

"You do that a lot, you know?" She felt slight and soft and incredibly warm against him. "You say no in a hundred different ways. But your eyes…they always say yes. It's been driving me crazy."

So did the sweet press of her breasts and the rapid-fire beat of her heart against his chest.

"Sorry, Doc. But I've just got to do this," he said and lowered his head.

He hadn't planned this when he'd come into town. Hadn't even planned it when he'd tugged her off the dance floor. He'd just known he wanted to see her again. And when he finally had, all he could think of was getting her alone. And now that he had her where he wanted her, the only thing he could think about was kissing her.

And man, oh, man, once his mouth touched hers, all he could think about was why had he waited so long. As he covered her lips with his, felt her stiffen, then soften, then open in response, he knew it was exactly the right thing to do.

She was too honest to fake resistance. Too much woman to ignore her own need. And while he was the one who'd initiated the kiss, she was the one who took things to another level and damn near brought him to his knees in the process.

Her fingers tightened on his biceps where at first she'd pushed away. Her body melted into his, pressed against him as she stretched up on her tiptoes, deepening the kiss, increasing the contact. The urgent upward slide of her body against his created the most incredible friction as her breasts brushed his chest and her stomach slid against an erection he didn't even attempt to hide.

With a triumphant groan, he lifted her off her feet and pinned her up against the wall of the building, wild to get closer, crazy to experience all that pliant heat. When he felt her hands in his hair, a moan rumbled up from deep in his chest. He slid his tongue inside her mouth. And damned near went up in flames.

Hot, wet silk. Honeyed and sweet. The taste of her was enough to make a strong man weak. And when her tongue darted out to meet his, the flames licking through his belly sparked an air-stealing inferno of need.

Sweet, sweet heaven. He felt consumed by her. Her heat. Her taste. Her reckless response that sent his heart-beat off the charts and pumped the blood from his head to his groin. He ground his hips against her, slid a hand down her bottom and lower, to cup the back of her knee and lift until her calf hooked his thigh and his hand slid up and under her skirt.

He heard her gasp, felt her shudder as he found bare skin, the bottom edge of lacy panties—then head-clearing pain as her fingers fisted in his hair and jerked his mouth away.

Five

Oh my God, Ali thought as she leaned back against the outside wall of the building, breathing hard, tugging down her skirt. John Tyler loomed above her, his face contorted in pain.

"What in the *hell* did you do that for?" he ground out as he rubbed his scalp.

"I wanted—I wanted you to stop."

At least she *should* have wanted him to stop. And that's why she'd pulled him away. Because she hadn't wanted him to. She'd wanted his kiss to go on and on and it had scared her.

"Well, hell, darlin'. One simple word would have done it. You didn't need to scalp me."

"I'm sorry," she said, embarrassed, breathless. But mostly turned on. And that was the part that alarmed her the most.

"I—I've got to go." With a frantic punch of panic, she hurried back into the Dusk to Dawn. And headed straight for the "Mares" room.

She turned on the tap, ran cold water over her wrists, then rubbed a wet, cold hand over the back of her neck. Finally, she let out a breath, faced herself in the mirror.

She looked like a woman who had been well and truly kissed. Her lips were swollen. Her eyes looked a little out of focus. And her face was flushed all the way down to her breasts—like a teenager who'd been making out in the backseat of a car.

She *felt* like a teenager—all raging hormones and fluttering heart.

What on earth was wrong with her? It was one thing to let him catch her off guard and kiss her. It was another to kiss him back. With enthusiasm.

And, oh, could that man kiss.

A sharp, electric ache spread from the tips of her breasts to low in her belly at the memory of his fingers on her bare thigh, under her skirt, rimming the edge of her panties.

She braced her hands on the edge of the sink, hung her head and rode through the rush.

This wasn't her. She didn't kiss men in the dark.

But she just had.

She shouldn't want to.

And yet...she did.

The unsettling knowledge that she'd wanted to do a whole lot more—*might* have done a whole lot more right there against the wall of a bar if she hadn't experienced a random moment of sanity—absolutely mortified her.

She had to get out of here. She had to get home. She had to think. She had to figure out what was happening to her.

But most of all, she had to deal with the sinking and sobering sense that she had very nearly committed the ultimate act of betrayal.

It was barely 9:00 a.m. on Monday and already the temperature had spiked up to the low eighties with a high around ninety-five expected. The county was clearly in the middle of a July heat wave—which was why John decided to make another trip into Sundown. Well, that and a blond veterinarian who had kissed him senseless Saturday night behind the Dusk to Dawn before trying to relieve him of most of his hair.

"That stretch of fence on the north range ain't gonna fix itself."

John grinned at the disapproval in Clive Johnson's voice. The only way to know if his grizzled old foreman was upset or good with the world was by his tone and the glint or glare from his rheumy old eyes. Currently, Clive was giving John both the glint *and* the glare plus a healthy helping of his guilt tone.

The confirmed bachelor had been John's father's foreman on the Bar T since buffalos roamed the foothills. In fact, his thin face looked like a piece of buffalo hide that had been soaked in a stream, wrung tight, then left to bake brown and bone-dry in the sun. John was relatively certain Clive's face had petrified long ago because in all the years he'd known him, he'd never seen him change his facial expression.

"Tomorrow, when it's supposed to be cooler, will be soon enough to tackle that fence," he told him when the old boy's evil eye locked on him like a laser beam.

"'Specially when there's skirts to chase today," Clive sputtered.

"Got that right." John gave Clive a good-natured clap on the back as he walked by him on the way to his truck. "You ought to try it some time. Mable Clemmons down at the post office asked about you again the other day," John teased, then laughed out loud when a flush of red lit up the tips of Clive's ears.

"Woman's a busybody and a know-it-all."

"Yeah but I hear tell she makes a mean pot roast."

"I can get by just fine without that woman's roast, thank ya very much…just like I can get by without that smart punk mouth a yours, boy."

"You live for my smart punk mouth. Gives you something to grumble about."

Clive snorted, then on cue, grumbled under his breath.

Chuckling, John climbed behind the wheel. "Take the

day off. And that's an order. Go on into town. Sling bull with your cronies at the Dusk to Dawn for a while. Tell 'em what a no-count lazy good-for-nothing my daddy raised. It'll make you feel better."

When Clive merely grunted again, John shook his head. He knew Clive didn't think of him that way but he enjoyed a good argument every bit as much as he enjoyed a sit-down with a beer and his old buddies at Sundown's one and only restaurant and bar. Trouble was, Clive didn't see a little R and R every once in a while as a necessity.

John knew different...especially where Clive was concerned.

"It's not a crime to take a little time off now and again. Enjoy it. I know I plan to."

Clive was still standing by the machine shed, watching him, when John pulled out on the gravel road.

"Status quo," he said under his breath and gunned the motor. He loved that stubborn old coot like he was blood family and he knew the feeling was mutual. Knew also that while he'd never explained to Clive why he sometimes shut himself up or rode off for days without a word, the old boy understood and didn't pry. John respected that and appreciated the distance Clive gave him. Just like he respected that Clive was one of the old breed. He didn't know anything but work, didn't feel comfortable unless he was working. Together, they *did* work. And they worked hard. But the old wrangler was slowing down and it was much easier to get Clive to ease up if John provided the reason.

Too hot was a good enough reason in any playbook.

Yeah, he thought as he barreled into town. Today was too hot to work, too hot to fish, but darn near perfect for paying a call on his favorite vet to see if she was dealing with some of the residual effects of a kiss that had heated him up like the sun beating down on the roof of his truck.

"Ladies." John tipped his hat to Peg and Ali as he walked into Ali's office. He knew from Peg that Ali held small-animal clinic on Monday mornings, so he'd counted on catching her at the office. He'd also picked up that Peg, who kept the books for her father's elevator and feed business in Sundown, made a habit of meeting Ali for lunch a couple of days a week. He'd kind of been hoping that today wouldn't have been one of them. Unfortunately, his luck hadn't held on that count.

"Hey, J.T." Peg's gaze was rampant with speculation as it flitted between him and Ali.

"Hi," Ali said, glancing up from her lunch. And looking very, very nervous.

For a woman who claimed not to be interested, she had the most extreme reactions around him. Of course, he did a little reacting of his own. And right now, it was appreciative silence.

She'd pulled her hair back into a utilitarian braid that started at the crown of her head and fell in a heavy rope to touch just between her shoulder blades. A stethoscope hung around her neck. She was dressed in working khaki pants and a matching shirt and running shoes.

A long look confirmed that she wasn't wearing a speck of makeup.

There wasn't one thing about her that didn't say business professional—except for the deepening pink flush on her cheeks that told him exactly what he'd wanted to know. She was thinking about the kiss they'd shared Saturday night out back of the Dusk to Dawn.

He'd never seen anything so sexy in his life. Or so sweet. And when her pained smile wavered somewhere between hesitancy and embarrassment, he knew she'd been thinking about that kiss as much as he had. Which meant she'd been thinking about it a lot.

"What brings you to town, J.T.?"

Leave it to Peg to try to force the obvious. She knew darn well why he was here—the reason was sitting there looking expectant and uncomfortable. No matter. He had it covered.

He dug into his shirt pocket. "Mom came through. She e-mailed these yesterday so I printed them for you. Thought you'd want them right away."

He tossed the packet of paper on the counter. As he'd hoped, the wariness left her eyes to be replaced by anticipation.

She rose, dusting her fingers on her pants and unfolded the pages.

"Oh, these are wonderful!" Eyes wide with excitement, she thumbed through the prints he'd made of the photographs of her house in its prime many years ago. "Peg—look. They're of my house. Oh, my gosh, look at this one. The hummingbird window is intact. I can have the replacement glass work done now to match it."

Peg, all narrowed eyes and curious look, rose, too, and peered over Ali's shoulder. "That's awfully thoughtful of you, J.T.," she said, her smile beaming. "So what's in it for you?"

Ali's head came up. Her blue eyes met his—a little wild, a lot self-conscious. Her blush returned, so pretty he couldn't help but smile.

"Cookies," he said, holding her gaze until the corners of her mouth finally tipped up in response. "I believe there's a promise on the table involving cookies."

"So there is," Ali said softly. "I'll get right on that."

"See you around, ladies," he said, liking the playful light that had entered her eyes. If Peg hadn't been there, he might have insisted on a retainer toward Ali's promise. Not cookies, but something just as sweet.

Instead, he touched his fingers to his hat, cut a quick goodbye look at Peg and walked out the door.

Ali studied the recipe, reviewing the list of ingredients. Flour, sugar, soda, salt, eggs, butter, oatmeal, raisins and nuts.

"Okay. That ought to do it," she said to herself and pulled out her big mixing bowl and mixer. "The man wants cookies. He's going to get cookies."

And it didn't mean one darn thing, she assured herself, measuring out the flour. He'd done a nice thing for her and she was merely paying him back.

With cookies.

When she caught herself smiling, she rolled her eyes, sobered up and tended to business. She'd promised him cookies and she was going to deliver so he'd know she was a woman of her word. And so he wouldn't have a reason to drop by unannounced and remind her that she owed him.

Or to kiss her. Like he'd kissed her Saturday night.

She let out a deep breath.

And really, really wished she understood what was happening to her.

But she didn't—at least she didn't want to admit she did—so she baked cookies.

Baking gave her something to do tonight. It was Saturday night. The night she and David used to set aside as their special date night. Even after the deepest cut of grief had healed, she still had trouble with Saturday nights.

Her fix had always been to treat it as any other night. She'd cocoon herself in a numbing little shell where the loss didn't affect her. And sometimes, it actually worked.

Tonight, however, wasn't one of those nights. Tonight was a night that if she started drinking wine, she'd have a hard time stopping. Tonight, the loneliness was crushing…maybe more so because John had made it clear she no longer needed to spend her nights alone.

It was not an option.

So, she baked instead. She baked to pass the time and

to forget what she missed, to block the emptiness that always hovered at the edge of her existence and would overtake her if she let it.

She'd just taken the last batch of cookies out of the oven when she heard a knock on her front door. She glanced at the clock. It was almost 8:00 pm. She wasn't expecting anyone. And when she realized she was actually hoping it might be John, she muttered in self-disgust and headed toward the door.

Wiping her hands on a dish towel, she walked through the dining room—which actually looked pretty good, she decided, admiring the results of her hard work—and opened the front door.

And there he stood. In all his heartthrob glory—tight-fitting jeans, black chest-hugging t-shirt and matching Resistol. His boots looked new. His smile was vintage flirt and, of course, he looked incredible.

"Hey, Doc. Thought you might be hungry."

Her shoulders sagged—even as her heart lifted like she was actually glad to see him.

Lord, give me strength.

The smell wafting out of the Dusk to Dawn carry-out sack made her stomach growl. She hadn't bothered with dinner. Hadn't had much of an appetite, as a matter of fact, until he'd shown up.

"So...are you? Hungry?" he added with an inviting grin.

She hung onto the side of the door. "You are the most persistent man."

"It's as endearing as hell, huh?"

What else could she do but smile. "Endearing is not exactly the word I would have chosen but we won't go there." She notched her chin toward the sack. "What's in the bag?"

"Burgers and fries. Best in the county."

"Do you know how much fat is in that stuff?" She was grasping at straws.

"Enough to clog the arteries of a small army." He waggled the bag under her nose. "Come on. Live dangerously."

Oh, she was. She definitely was.

She drew in a deep whiff. Suppressed a moan of pleasure.

"You want it bad, don't you?"

"Oh, yeah," she confessed. "I do. You'd just as well come on in. As long as you're here, you can take your cookies home with you."

"You baked me cookies?" He sounded genuinely surprised and pleased.

"I said I would."

"Actually, you said you'd *show* me your cookies."

The man truly was incorrigible. "So I did."

She led him into the kitchen, pointed to the counter where she'd spread the cookies out to cool. "Take a good look because these are the only cookies of mine you're ever going to see."

He chuckled. "Is this conversation getting silly or what?"

"Or what," she agreed. "It's been a long day."

"And you're obviously food-deprived. Sit. I'll set the table. They smell great, by the way." He nodded toward the cookies and somehow managed to lean in close and sniff her neck. "So do you. Like vanilla."

She hoped she hadn't jumped as she moved toward a chair and sat down. She must have, though, because he was sporting a smug grin as he opened the bag and set a tissue-wrapped burger, a container of fries and a takeout cup full of soda in front of her.

"Dinner is served."

Dinner. Well. He'd done it again, hadn't he? He'd managed to maneuver her into eating with him. At this point, she was too hungry to point out that she was on to his tactics. Big whoop. Being on to him was a far cry from knowing how to handle him—especially since she thought about that kiss at the darnedest times. Like when she was in the shower or brushing her teeth or…okay, almost always.

And the other thing—the thing that really knocked the pins out from under her—she really *was* happy to see him.

He made her feel something other than empty.

What was she going to do about this man?

Ali knew it was dangerous to get so comfortable with him, but by the end of the evening, she was. And she no longer had it in her to fight the feeling. He had a talent for making her smile and laugh and forget why she should be resisting him.

They'd polished off their burgers and fries and she'd packed up his cookies—after he'd eaten half a dozen, all the while telling her he deserved another batch minimum for bringing her dinner tonight.

She hadn't bought the argument, but she'd had fun bantering back and forth with him until somehow, it had gotten to be ten o'clock. He'd made noises about leaving but while they'd made it as far as her front porch, he hadn't made any moves toward his truck.

The porch swing had been too inviting. He sat on one end, she on the other, pleasantly full and a little too relaxed to keep her guard up. Of course, it helped that he talked about silly things like stories of life on the ranch with his old bachelor foreman, Clive Johnson.

Ali had met Clive the first time she'd made a ranch visit.

"I don't think he approved of me as a vet."

"Clive doesn't approve of much of anything," he said with a lazy smile. "So don't let it bother you."

The affection in his tone undercut any censure. "You care a lot about him, don't you?"

"Yeah. He's an ornery old coot, but he's my ornery old coot and I can't imagine life without his grumbling."

The chain holding the swing from the porch ceiling creaked softly as they rocked back and forth in a lazy rhythm.

"I could fix that for you," he said looking up and inspecting the chain.

"The squeak? No. It's fine. I like it. It's…comfortable."

For a few moments more they simply sat there, the

chain creaking, soft music drifting through the open windows from the CD player she'd turned on midway through their burgers and fries. And she felt content.

"Who is that?" John asked, cocking an ear toward the screen door. "I don't think I've heard her before."

Ali's favorite CD had just made the rotation on her CD changer. "Norah Jones."

"Silk," he said after listening for a while longer. "Yeah…like water flowing over silk. I like it."

Ali nodded into the dark, taken by his comment. "Good analogy. She's very smooth."

"And this particular song is perfect to dance to."

She turned and searched his face. Shook her head when she read his intentions.

"Oh, no. You've seen me dance. If I remember right, you took a lot of pleasure in insulting me about how terrible I am," she reminded him with a lift of a brow.

"Not terrible. Just—okay. I can't lie. You are terrible." He smiled to take the sting out of his teasing. "Now's a great time to fix that."

"Many have tried."

"*I* haven't." He rose and drew her to her feet with him.

She was still shaking her head when he pulled her into his arms.

"Quiet. Just listen. That's it. Listen to the music. Feel the beat. And relax, Doc. Just relax."

Right. *That* was going to happen. She was dancing in the dark, wrapped in the arms of approximately two hundred pounds of hard, hot cowboy who made no bones about the fact that he wanted to do a lot more than dance with her. And see her cookies.

"Close your eyes," he murmured, lowering his head until his lips hovered a breath away from her ear. "And just sway with me. We'll worry about the footwork later. For now, just let out that breath you're holding and go with the flow."

Flow. Oh, yes. She had a lot of flowing going on if the slip-slide of her blood thrumming through her veins was any indication. Every pressure point where her body nudged up against his let her know about flow. His breath, where it feathered across her temple like a caress, set all of her juices flowing.

The front of her thighs brushed against the front of his, all hard, long muscle and tensile strength. The tips of her breasts grazed his chest and tightened into sensitive little pressure points. And his hands…Lord, his hands had folded together at the small of her back, exerting the slightest, yet most intense pressure she'd ever known.

Flow. The only thing that didn't seem to be surging through her at the moment was cognizant thought. And at the moment, she couldn't quite make herself care.

The music was soft and low. The man was hard and lean. And the incredible, enveloping sensation of being held and touched and gently nudged to move with the heady, sensual rhythm of the music not only comforted, it consumed.

He held her loosely yet so intimately she was aware of everything different and everything the same about them. He was tall, she was small. He was hard, she was soft. But through their veins, rivers of lifeblood flowed, powering their hearts, fueling their muscles, pulsing in places that made awareness of each other mandatory and denial a pretty tough feat.

The scent of the night—honeysuckle and sage—melded with the scent of his skin which she'd come to recognize as a tantalizing mix of musk and leather and something unique to only him.

It felt natural now, swaying in the dark against him. He made it so easy for her move her feet as he gently nudged her forward, then back, then in a slow, rhythmic circle. Made it so easy to lose herself in the moment. And easier still to wonder about other moments. The ones she'd missed. The ones he wanted.

The ones she just couldn't bring herself to invite or encourage.

"That's it," he murmured against her temple, "You've got it. Feel that?"

Everything. She felt everything.

Including regret that he so easily made her want what she'd never imagined wanting again.

"There you go. Simple as pie, right?"

She couldn't answer. Didn't want to hear her own voice in the dark with this man who wanted her to let go of things she'd clung to with the fierceness of a warrior.

Memories. Promises. The man who had made her a woman. A wife.

"It's…it's getting late," she said, pulling out of his

arms. And feeling very cold suddenly even though the summer night held the lingering warmth of the July day.

For a long moment, he said nothing. He just stood there. She could feel his gaze on the top of her head. Feel his disappointment in the long breath fanning her cheek.

"Well," he said finally, his voice sounding gritty. "I'd better go home so you can go to bed."

She gave him a tight, clipped smile and wrapped her arms around her waist. "Don't forget your cookies."

One corner of that beautiful mouth tipped up. "Not likely.

"See ya 'round, Doc," he said, sauntering down her porch steps toward his truck.

"Thanks for dinner." She walked up to her porch post and hung on.

Without breaking stride or turning around, he touched his fingers to his hat brim and kept right on going.

So did her heartbeat.

Reminding her, again, how very alive she truly was. How very alive he made her feel.

Six

"It's more complicated than that," Ali insisted the following Monday when Peg dropped by the clinic with her lunch.

Peg lifted a forkful of salad, pointed it at Ali. "There's nothing complicated about good old-fashioned lust."

She hadn't intended to tell Peg about this shift in her feelings about John Tyler but, in the end, Peg hadn't even had to wheedle it out of her. What was the point? When she'd left the welcome party early, begging off with a headache, and then when John had shown up at the clinic last Monday all sexy grins and talk about cookies, it hadn't taken Peg long to put two and two together and know there was something in the wind.

"Wait a minute. He kissed you, didn't he?"

"Oh, yeah," Ali had confessed without so much as a token denial and then knuckled under and spilled all the details—including how John had showed up at her house a week later with burgers and fries and taught her how to dance in the dark.

She hadn't realized how badly she wanted to talk about it. Now she couldn't stop talking about it.

"The thing is," Ali confided thoughtfully, "I'm so utterly shocked that I feel this attraction to him. Not just to him—to any man."

"John's not just any man."

"Tell me about it. According to you he's fast and loose and way too freethinking about sex and…and… well, I shouldn't like him, but I do. And I don't want to. I just don't want to."

Peg pulled a face but Ali kept right on rambling.

"In the first place he *is* too young, that's just a fact. Besides, he's not my type. He's never been my type. Never will be. But most of all, I don't want to get involved. With anyone."

"But?" Peg asked, knowing there was a qualifier.

Ali let out a pained breath. "But…he makes me want things and I—I just don't know how to handle it."

"It?"

"*It.* Everything." She was quiet for a while as she contemplated the ham sandwich she'd made for her lunch. It had sounded good this morning. Now, somehow, she'd lost her appetite.

She stood, shoved her hands in her hip pockets and walked to the window overlooking Main Street. Pickup trucks lined the south side of the street where an equipment auction was taking place at the implement dealers.

"I know this sounds clichéd, " she began slowly, "but when David died, it really felt like part of me died, too, you know? I loved that man. He was steady and solid and he was my best friend. We grew up together—literally. Our houses were next door to each other. Our parents were best friends. Until four years ago, I didn't have a memory that didn't include him. And I have never once, in all the years since I lost him, considered getting involved with another man."

"Because it seems like a betrayal," Peg offered gently.

Ali turned, looked at her friend, not really surprised by her insight. "Yeah. It feels like a betrayal."

"Would David want you to be alone?"

Ali shook her head. "This isn't about what David would have wanted. It's about what I want."

"And what is it you want, sweetie?"

Ali stared at the ceiling. "I want to do a good job here, build my practice, build a life—on my own."

"And yet…John reminds you that you have needs that you hadn't factored into the equation."

She closed her eyes. Felt a burst of sexual awareness shiver through her. Boy, did he remind her. "Do you suppose it's just an age thing?" she asked when the thought suddenly came to her. "You know, I've read where women reach their sexual peak in their late thirties, early forties. Do you suppose this is all about hormones kicking in?"

"Well," Peg said sympathetically, "I suppose if you're looking for an excuse, that's as good a one as any."

"I'm not looking for an excuse," Ali insisted, feeling defensive. "I'm looking for an explanation."

"I think," Peg said gently, "that what you're really looking for is absolution."

Ali wanted to argue but not enough to stop listening to what else Peg had to say.

"I think," Peg continued when she saw she had Ali's attention, "that you are an attractive, healthy, sexual woman and somewhere along the line you decided you didn't have the right to be any of those things. And you were good with that—at least you made yourself be good with it until J.T. gave you a reason to question that decision."

"I don't live in a vacuum, Peg. There have been other men who've made it known they were interested. I didn't have this problem with them."

"Maybe you just weren't ready. Or maybe they weren't J.T."

The phone rang about that time and ended their discussion. Ali had to rush out to the Savage spread to treat a colicky colt. The ride out to Lee and Ellie Savage's place gave her a chance to think about what Peg had said.

"Like you haven't been thinking about it day and night," she muttered as she bounced along the gravel road toward Shiloh Ranch.

For the rest of the day, she was too busy to think about John or his kiss or his smiles or his dancing or anything else, for that matter. After she got the Savage's colt back on his feet and out of trouble, she headed across country to the Grangers' to do some herd testing for the state lab. In fact, she had a whole list of stops to make yet that afternoon.

By the time she finally made it home, it was well after sunset.

By the time she finally made it to bed, she was too exhausted to think.

But it didn't stop her from dreaming. And when she dreamed, she dreamed not of David as she had so many, many nights since she'd lost him. She dreamed of John Tyler instead. She dreamed of that kiss. Of how kissing him had made her feel alive. And as needy as she'd felt needed.

The next morning, as she lay awake and alone in her bed, still achy from the vivid aftermath of the dream, she couldn't help but question if maybe Peg was right.

Maybe she *was* looking for absolution. Maybe she was even looking for permission. To be a woman again. To feel the kind of intense physical pleasure a hot, steamy affair with a younger man could bring.

And that's all it could ever be between them. David had been her one and only love. She didn't harbor any delusions that she'd find what she'd had with him with another man.

An affair.

"Whoa."

She sat up in bed, braced her fists on the mattress beside her hips. The idea was so far beyond the realm of anything she'd consider appropriate there weren't words to explain it. And yet…John Tyler certainly had jump-started her hormones and had her thinking in that direction.

It was ridiculous. It would be too complicated, and just thinking about it brought on such strong feelings of guilt, she wasn't certain she could enjoy it even if she did have the courage to see it through.

And when had her thoughts started swaying more in the direction of seeing it through than nipping it in the bud?

Since John had backed her up against a wall and kissed her, that's when.

Since pretty much all she could think about was what it would feel like to have him kiss her again.

Since he'd taken her cookies and left her on her front porch Saturday night without so much as a peck on the cheek and she'd had to latch on to the porch post with both hands so she wouldn't chase him down the sidewalk and demand that, for God's sake, he kiss her again.

Urggh.

If she *didn't* kiss him again, she had the ominous feeling that she was going to jump out of her skin.

"It's going well, huh?"

Ali frowned at Peg, then cast an overt glance toward John where he and Cutter and Lee Savage were standing together over a barbecue grilling steaks and doing what men did best, laughing and giving each other a hard time.

"Define well."

Peg laughed and handed her a stack of plates loaded with silverware. "You're doing fine. Set the table. It'll give you something to do with your hands other than wring them."

Ali was on a date. A *date,* for heaven's sake. Well, not a *date* date, at least not technically, but it didn't change the fact that she was here and John was here and she'd agreed to come to this get-together at Peg and Cutter's knowing full well the motive for it.

"It'll be perfect," Peg had insisted when she'd called and cooked this up. "It'll be you and John, Cutter and me and we'll ask Lee and Ellie Savage over, too. Friday night. We'll have a cookout. Just a bunch of friends getting together. It'll give you a chance to get to know him better."

"I don't want to get to know him," Ali had said grimly. "I just want to jump his bones."

Peg's laugh was big and surprised. "Well, I'll say this for you, girl. When you decide to turn over a new leaf, you do it in a big way."

"That was a joke."

"No, it wasn't."

Sadly, Peg had been right—even though Ali was hard pressed to admit it in her more sane moments. Agreeing to this event hadn't been one of them, she thought now, as she distributed tableware around the picnic table and tried to keep from looking at John. Second thoughts had moved in and paid rent the moment she'd made the decision to harken to the call of her hormones, so to speak.

And now, here she was. Harkening.

It was exhausting.

She hadn't paid this much attention to her hair and makeup in ages. And she hadn't felt this nervous in decades. Probably since junior high—which was laughable appropriate since more and more often lately she felt like she was functioning with the mentality of a teenager.

She glanced at the men again—and stopped breathing when she realized John was watching her. His expression was sober, his gaze assessing and intent. And when his brown eyes, as warm as melted chocolate, locked on hers and one corner of his incredible mouth tilted up in a private, intimate smile, her heart went haywire.

She was not a strong swimmer and as she looked away from his July-hot gaze, busying herself with rearranging plates on the picnic table, she had a vivid mental image of herself drifting toward deep water and sinking fast.

Oh, God. What had she been thinking?

As he shot the breeze with Cutter and Lee, John drained his bottle of beer and tried not to make a production out of watching every move Ali made. His mind wasn't tracking one hundred percent of what the guys were saying. It was getting to be an old story but the doc pretty much occupied the bulk of his thoughts.

He found it interesting that he couldn't quite get a bead on why she, of all women, had him so hot and bothered. Yeah, she was a gorgeous woman. He knew a lot of gorgeous women, though, many of whom liked the idea of him taking them to dinner or to a movie. At last count not a one of them had attempted to relieve him of his hair. Or baked him cookies, he reminded himself with a grin.

Ali fascinated him. Something unsettling had happened when he'd held her close against him that night on her front porch. Something electric and consuming. She'd felt like a little piece of heaven in his arms and the look in her eyes when she'd pulled away from him had rocked him. Heat. Desire. Need. Wavering denial. And panic. She wanted him. Just as badly as he wanted her but she was fighting it every step of the way.

Apparently, she was still fighting it because every time her blue eyes landed on him and she realized he was watching her, she quickly looked away. That was okay. Just gave him more room to watch her.

She'd dressed to accommodate the heat. Nothing overtly sexy—just a pale blue crop top that gave little peeks of bare skin where it almost met the waistband of her jeans shorts. A pair of leather sandals flip-flopped when she walked and made her legs look absolutely incredible.

It didn't seem to matter what she wore—on her anything looked sexy.

"You look like a man with a powerful thirst, J.T. Need another beer?"

Cutter's sly grin made it clear he thought he knew exactly what John had a thirst for and that beer wasn't going to quench it.

John never had and never did kiss and tell. And since there was no way he was going to get into any kind of discussion with Cutter about the doc, he headed for the cooler. "A beer'd be great. How about you, Lee?"

"Thanks." Lee Savage reached for the bottle when John handed it to him. The rancher who had married one of John's all-time favorite people, Ellie Shiloh, a few years back, eyed John beneath his hat brim. "So what's up with you and Alison?"

Okay. So they were both of a mind to give him grief. Or at least they were going to try. "Don't know what you're talking about," he lied then tightened his lips when Cutter made a choking sound.

After a few moments of amused consideration, Lee grunted. "In that case, you might want to put your tongue back in your mouth, because you're doing a fine imitation of a man going down for the count."

Hell, was he that obvious? Apparently so, because these two were grinning like a couple of goons. "Since when does appreciating a pretty woman equate to *going down for the count?* I'm sorry to disappoint you, boys, but the doc and I are just friends."

Cutter flipped a steak and grinned at Lee. "That's because she won't give him the time of day."

"Ouch. Met your match with this one, have you, J.T.?"

"Oh, he's way outmatched," Cutter said on a laugh.

"It's a little different playing to a classy woman instead of the party girls who go all limp-kneed over our favorite bachelor."

"Well, they can't all be conquests," Lee added with a total lack of sympathy.

"You two are too funny for words." Refusing to rise to the bait, John just grinned back. "It just busts your chops that you're missing out on the joys of single life. That's the problem with married men. Can't stand to see an unattached man enjoying all the freedom that goes with being single. Me, I like my life just the way it is— no strings attached, no ring in my nose to be led around by like some among us who shall remain nameless."

"It's your story, you can tell it any way you want to," Lee said, clearly unperturbed by John's ribbing, "but if I was a betting man, I'd say you aren't too happy about this *just friends* arrangement."

It would be easy to let them rile him—especially since they were right. He *wasn't* happy about it. But he knew something they didn't. He knew how the doc responded when he kissed her. He knew how she melted against him in the moonlight with a little help from Norah Jones. So, this *just friends* business was going to evolve into something a whole lot more pleasurable real soon. Hell, she was here tonight, wasn't she? That said something.

In the meantime, as far as going down for the count, his buddies couldn't be more off target. Oh, he intended to woo and win the good doctor, all right. Just like he intended for them both to have a good time in the process. But he knew his limits. Even his best friends and family didn't know about the side of him that had emerged since Afghanistan. No way was he subjecting a woman like Alison to that part of him. And no way was he letting himself open to the scrutiny.

Yeah, the big, tough happy-go-lucky cowboy was afraid he'd be found out. Afraid they'd discover he was a fraud. The head docs could babble on all they wanted about emotional scars being as disabling as physical ones but he knew it was all bunk. He had both his arms, he had both his legs. He was alive. And he ought to be damn happy about it, instead of cowering in the dark when the flashbacks got the best of him and shoved him in the black pit…sometimes for days.

"Something on your mind that you'd like to share with us, J.T.?"

John threw Cutter a tight smile. "Yeah. I was thinking the company over at the swing set has got to be a step up from the likes of you two jokers.

"Hey Shelby girl," he said, walking away from his buddies toward the Reno children. "How's it shakin', sweetheart? Yeah, I see you, little dude," he said on a laugh as two-year-old Dawson launched into a chorus of *J.T., J.T.* and toddled toward him at a baby bull trot.

"You can run but you can't hide." Cutter's laugh trailed after him as John walked away.

Yeah, he could run all right, he thought, scooping up Dawson and lifting him over his head until the two-year-old squealed with laughter. He'd been running and hiding for over a year and he wasn't changing the plan now.

It was how he kept himself in the game. It was how he stayed alive.

"I'll never get used to the sky out here," Ali said as she reclined on a chaise lounge in the Renos' back yard, staring heavenward. "It's so amazingly beautiful. Day or night."

"Yeah, it's a huge change from a city sky," John agreed, sitting beside her in a folding lawn chair. "It's one of the things I missed those years when…when I was gone."

The darkness was summer-soft, the sky a swath of velvet black glittering with the most incredible array of stars. A full moon hung like a dinner plate smack in the middle of it all.

Despite the fact that her nerves were pretty much frazzled from the tension zinging between her and John all evening, Ali drew from the beauty of the night to help to calm her.

And it did. But not much.

The Savages had said their goodbyes a few minutes ago. Shortly after that Peg and Cutter had excused themselves with a promise to be right back as they'd carried a sleeping Dawson and a played-out Shelby into the house to put them to bed.

Their disappearing act had been a little staged, conveniently leaving Ali and John alone together for the first time all evening.

She was running out of things to talk about. And she was desperate, suddenly, to keep the conversation impersonal and benign. They'd covered the Reno children, Ellie Savage's pregnancy, Cutter and Lee's joint bucking herd venture. When those lines of conversation dried up, the good old standby weather and state of the economy filled dead air until finally any attempt at small talk drifted away to nothing and there was no avoiding that they were very, very much alone together.

Yes, she was here. Yes, she'd agreed to Peg's orchestrated effort to get her and John together. But that had been before—that nebulous *before* when the prospect had been far enough away that she hadn't had to deal with it until later. Now it was *later.* Now it was *now.* And *now,* she really couldn't believe she'd agreed to this almost date.

God.

"Can I ask you something, Doc?"

Ali's heart rate ratcheted up a couple beats per minute when John's deep voice split the silence and reminded her just how *now* it was.

She felt his gaze on her, considering, questioning. "Sure."

"I've been wondering…are we on a date tonight?"

The straightforwardness of his question didn't surprise her. He wasn't stupid. But she was. Stupid and embarrassed. Were forty-year-old women supposed to feel this way? Fluttery and flustered and so strung out on sexual tension she had to wrap her fingers around the arm of the chaise to keep them from trembling?

"Ali?"

She let out a long breath, stalled the inevitable a little longer. "Do people still do that? Date?"

Again, those dark eyes studied her in the night. "Some do, yeah."

"Well," she said and gave up, knowing she couldn't evade the issue any longer. "Then I guess you could say we're on one."

His thoughtful silence added to her tension. "Interesting," he finally said.

She stared up at the sky. "I thought so, too."

When he spoke again, his voice was as soft and deep as the darkness. "Does this mean you're reconsidering *dinner*?"

Dinner. Well, as euphemisms went, she supposed it was fitting in their case. All she had to do was look at him and she felt a hunger so consuming it made her ache. But still, it was the million-dollar question. She might want *dinner* with him, but he wasn't talking about pizza or burgers and fries. He was talking about a full-course meal. So to speak.

"The jury's still out," she admitted because it was the truth and because she felt he was entitled to know she was still uncertain about the idea of a love affair. Her heart jumped again, just admitting that an affair was what they were talking about.

He leaned forward in his chair, propped his elbows

on his spread thighs and contemplated his clasped hands. "Well, at least I haven't been found guilty and sentenced to hang yet."

"Good old frontier justice," she said unable to stop a smile. "It was so effective and simple."

"This—you and me—could be very simple." His gaze held hers across a few feet of moonlight. "You're the one who's making things complicated."

Yeah. She was. She knew she was.

"Look, Doc, you know that I think you're incredible. I haven't made any bones about it, or that I'm interested in getting to know you better. It doesn't get any less complicated than that." He lifted a hand, a gesture that said *look at me.* "And neither do I. I'm just a good old boy. Out for a good time. That's all I need to make me happy. Now what could possibly be wrong with that?"

Everything. And nothing. "Not a thing. If you're you."

"Ah." A sage nod. "But you're not me."

"Not even close."

"But you want to be," he concluded, nodding his head as if he'd just figured out a complex equation. "At least you want to be more *like* me."

She could lie. But what was the point. "Maybe. Sure. I'd love to know what it was like to do what, well, what we're talking about for nothing more than the sake of a good time. Problem is, it also puts me at odds with who I am."

"Okay," he said slowly, "let's start there. Who are you, Alison Samuels? Who are you that you won't let your-

self have what you want? And why won't you let yourself have it? Does it scare you so much? Do *I* scare you?"

"You…um…you don't beat about the bush, do you?"

He shrugged. "Life's short. Why waste time?"

Life *was* short. She knew it better than anyone. The
love of her life was gone, his short life taken way too
soon. She hadn't been able to save him. Hadn't been
able to stop his death from happening.

But she could do something about *her* life. Did she
intend to miss out on an experience like John Tyler because she was so mired in what *was* that she couldn't
see her way clear to what could be?

Would it really be so wrong to let this man ease some
of the ache? Fill some of the void? As long as they both
knew going in that was the extent of it? Nothing long-
term. No fear of losing in the end. Because that, she realized as she sat there with this beautiful man watching
her and making it clear that he wanted her, was the real
threat. She couldn't risk loving anyone again. It hurt too
much to lose them.

But she could *like* someone, couldn't she? Like
them, have some fun with them, fill a few lonely hours
with them?

She looked up into his eyes. "Maybe," she began, her
heart suddenly hammering at her boldness, "you do
scare me. Maybe the prospect of having *dinner* with you
scares me. But, maybe I've also reached a point in my
life where I agree with your philosophy and would like
very much to grasp it."

"And yet you can't quite get yourself to make the leap."

"I'm working on it."

"What can I do to bring you all the way over to my side?" His smile was open and curious. "I have needs. You have needs. Surely, they don't stray that far from each other. Again, pretty simple."

He paused again, looked at her. "Simple unless your idea of simple has always been a nice, safe, black-and-white life. No wild rides. No chance of having too good of a time because, well, hell, that might be risky."

He just kept surprising her. His intellect. His insight.

She laughed because what else was there to do. "Seems like you have me all figured out."

He made a self-deprecating sound. "God, I hope not. That would take all the fun out of getting to know you."

"Tell me what you see anyway," she said, inviting him to elaborate. "I can take it. I think."

He whipped his head her way, probed her eyes in the starlit night. "I see a beautiful, intelligent woman who takes herself way too seriously. You need to loosen up, Doc. Live *in* life, not outside of it."

It felt like she'd been hit in the head with a brick. My God. He was right. He was so right. Since David had died, she had been living outside of life. Living in it had been too painful. Now it was starting to feel painful on the outside.

Still… "There are very few guarantees your way."

"Oh, sweetheart, you want guarantees? Not gonna

happen. Not in this life—inside or outside of it. That's part of the risk. It's also part of the reward."

"And part of the reason I've turned my back on certain…aspects of my life," she said, realizing it for the first time but feeling steadier somehow because of his frank openness. "Maybe you've convinced me that I should at least rethink things."

A smile crept over his face. "Things? Like dinner?"

"Yes. Like *dinner.* Why don't you ask me again. We'll see what happens from there."

He narrowed his eyes playfully. "You're not setting me up for another letdown, are you? I mean, all I've gotten so far is a pickup load of big fat rejections. Not to mention you damn near ripped my scalp off."

"I really am sorry about that. It was knee-jerk, you know? I guess you could say I panicked."

"And now? No more panic?"

She pushed out a laugh. "Oh, I wouldn't say that, exactly."

"What would you say?"

"I'd say, if you're not going to ask me, I guess I'll just have to ask you. Would you like to go out to dinner some night?"

Another long, probing look. "You're sure about this?"

"Absolutely not," she admitted then took the big plunge. "But what I am sure about is that you've blurred a few of the lines I'd drawn in my neat and tidy little rule book."

He pushed out a soft chuckle. "Thank God, because

you've been playing fast and loose with some of my lines, too."

"Really?" She felt and sounded a little breathless as she watched him hitch himself out of his chair, then settle a hip beside her on the chaise.

She made room for him by drawing her knees toward her chest. The man didn't waste any time. He made her all shivery and aware of the dangerous territory she was about to enter when he covered her knees with his hand.

"Really," he whispered, bending in close and sliding his hand the length of her outer thigh until he cupped her hip, squeezed.

Anticipation thrummed through her blood and increased her level of sensitivity until her nerve endings were singing.

"What do you say," he murmured, his lips hovering a breath away from hers, "wanna see if we can muddy up a few more of those lines?"

Seven

Her lines were already good and muddied, thank you very much, but Ali had invited this so she'd better be prepared to follow through. And maybe, just maybe, another kiss would take the mystique out of the first one, downgrade the fascination and show them both there wasn't really all that much to get fired up about.

She didn't hold out a lot of hope for a letdown. In fact, she was pretty certain another kiss was just going to leave her wanting more.

The chaise was soft and giving against her back. His hand was strong and possessive as he moved it to her waist. And the scent of him—summer warmth woven with musk and leather—filled her senses to bursting as she waited in suspended animation.

She supposed she should say something…something sexy and clever that would minimize the tension of the moment, downgrade it to what it was…a kiss. Just a kiss. But she'd never played this kind of game before. Flirting might come second nature to John, but she'd never had any practice at it. She must have made a sound though, because his beautiful mouth brushed against hers.

"I'll take that as a yes."

Well, umm…ya-ah.

His mouth met hers on a smile. Whimsically soft. Arousingly sensual. She lifted her hands to his chest, slid them slowly upward until they circled his neck and pulled him closer.

And then his arms were around her, dragging her away from the chaise, folding her against him—and *he* was the one making sounds of affirmation. A groan rumbled up from deep in his chest as he opened his mouth over hers and drew her into a kiss that didn't just blur the lines, it obliterated them.

So much for a downgrade.

The feel of his body against hers, hard and strong and hot, awakened not only the sensual memory of that first, consuming kiss, but the yearnings of a woman who'd missed the touch of a man, the taste of a man, the passion of a man who wanted her.

The hair at his nape was silky soft against her fingers, the skin there smooth and warm. His breath, feathering across her cheek as he changed the angle of his mouth, was hot and hurried.

She absorbed it all—the textures, the scent, the taste of him. But underlying it all was the most incredible sensation of being held by someone strong and vital, the powerful knowledge that this stunning young man not only wanted her, he was swept away with wanting her.

The sound of a door slamming in the darkness made her jump.

John tensed but held her tight. He drew a bracing breath, then slowly pulled away. "I think maybe someone just fired a warning shot," he murmured, touching his forehead to hers. "We're about to have company."

The tension in his muscled shoulders and the hesitancy with which he let her go belied his easy grin as he stood, leaving her sitting there, her lips tingling, her heartbeat hammering like crazy. And every erogenous zone in her body cranked up to overload.

"So, did you get the little ones all settled in?" she heard him ask through the ringing in her ears.

"They're down for the count." Peg's voice grew closer as she and Cutter joined them in the back yard.

"Time for me to head for the barn,, too," John said.

"It's Friday night," Peg protested. "What's the rush? I thought we'd crack open a bottle of wine and talk for a little while yet. "

Ali watched John shake his head. "Sorry, sweetie. Clive's got a full day planned tomorrow and if I don't hit the saddle with him by five o'clock, he'll be just stubborn enough to head out on his own."

"I've got to be going, too." Ali stood, glad for the dark that hid the flush on her cheeks.

"Well, heck," Peg said with a pretty pout. "And here I thought the night had just begun."

Cutter pulled her against his side and whispered something in her ear that made them both grin.

"Well, if you've got to go," Peg said brightly, "you've got to go."

"And don't let the gate hit your taillights on the way out," Cutter added.

John laughed. "Come on, Ali. I think they've just decided our company isn't so mandatory, after all. Thanks, guys. Everything was great."

"Yes. It was very nice. See you Monday for lunch, Peg?"

"Oh, you can count on it," Peg said, her smile brimming with curiosity.

"Come on." John touched a hand to her back and they left the Renos to their own devices. "I'll walk you to your car, then follow you home, make sure you get back all right."

"You don't have to do that."

"I want to," he said and satisfied that she was buckled in, walked on over to his truck.

All the way home, with John's headlights trailing her, Ali wondered what to expect when they arrived at her house.

Did she ask him in?

She shouldn't ask him in. That was the coward in her talking.

Maybe he wouldn't even want to come in. They were just talking about dinner sometime after all.

Right. Dinner. Not…*dinner.*

Although that kiss sure had her thinking about…*dinner.* A seven-course meal would be good.

Oh, God. Forty going on fourteen.

When they reached her house and he pulled up behind her, she'd decided it was time to be a grown-up about this. Nothing said they couldn't take this slow. Nothing said that just because they'd discussed possibilities that they had to act on them like a couple of kids revved on raging hormones.

She was just about to open her car door when it opened, and there he was, holding out a hand to help her out. She took it, hyperaware of the feel of his calloused palm and strong fingers encompassing hers.

On a deep breath, she rose and, hand in hand, they walked to her front door.

"So," he said, turning her to face him under the porch roof, "about that dinner. Will tomorrow night work? There's a great little Italian place in Bozeman…. That is, if you like Italian?"

"Italian's great. Wonderful," she said, when it all meshed for her that he really was talking about taking her out to eat. "And tomorrow night's good," she added when she realized the sound she'd been hearing in the background was his truck's motor running.

Relief would have been a little sweeter if disappointment hadn't taken a big bite out of it. He didn't have any intention of staying.

"Word to the wise, Doc," he said. "If you don't worry about tomorrow, it's a lot easier to enjoy today."

"Translated—live in the moment."

"You got it. G'nite." Leaning down, he pressed a chaste and very sweet kiss on her forehead.

"Good night," she murmured as he left her there on her porch wondering who, during the process of the night, had turned the tables on whom?

She let herself inside, turned on the foyer light and wandered slowly to the kitchen where she snagged a cookie out of a cookie jar shaped like a cow—a goodbye gift from her staff in K.C. Leaning back against the counter, she stood there munching, staring into space. It was a while before she realized she was smiling into the dark. What else could she do but smile?

She'd been here a month and John Tyler had been hitting on her on an average of once or twice a week. Tonight, she gotten up the nerve to let him know she might be interested in the same thing he was. One minute, he was kissing her senseless and the next he was giving her a brotherly peck and heading home to the range.

Was it all part of some grand plan, she wondered as she turned off lights, brushed her teeth and went to bed. Was the idea to keep her confused? Make her crazy?

Keep her on edge until she was so rattled and strung out with sexual tension that she took the initiative and dragged him off to bed by his belt buckle? Or was he truly being nice and giving her a chance to back out if she had a change of heart?

Okay. First things first. Her heart had nothing to do with this. Sure. She liked him but this wasn't about hearts. It was about satisfying needs. Needs she hadn't known she still had until John moved in and uncovered them like old bones on an archeological dig.

She growled low in her throat and flopped onto her stomach.

She was too old for all this turmoil. Growing old, as the saying goes, was mandatory. Growing *up,* evidently, was not. Well, she'd considered herself a grown-up for a good many years now until, once again, John had her thinking about necking in the back seat of the nearest car.

She'd have to be careful around him. Especially careful not to mistake the things she was feeling for him as anything but chemistry. She only had room in her life for one great love and he was gone. No amount of wishful thinking could change that.

"And?"

The doc's beautiful blue eyes opened slowly as she swallowed a bite of her tortellini carbonara with a blissful sigh. "And you were right. This is amazing. How did you find this place? And what's it doing in the middle of Montana?"

"A friend of mine owns it," John answered as he watched her enjoy her pasta. Eating appeared to be a sensual, celebratory experience for the good doctor. Her eyes were often closed, her breath was deep and slow as she savored every bite. In turn, it was a sensual experience watching her.

As far as that went, everything about her was sensual, from her sage blue eyes that made him think of sleepy mornings after, to her woman's curves and full lips that smiled dreamily as she enjoyed her meal.

She'd dressed up for him. He liked it. Liked the way her legs looked in those high, open-toed black heels, liked that she'd painted her toenails siren red and that she'd done a little something extra with her hair. The black decorative comb holding a sweep of blond silk behind her left ear matched her dress. A dress that looked a whole lot like a black slip with its thin straps and short hemline.

It was a summer dress and she'd worn it in deference to the heat. She might be cool in it, he thought, making himself take a sip of wine, but he'd been heating up by degrees ever since she'd met him at her door when he'd picked her up at seven to take her to Bozeman and Spaghetti Western.

"You have good friends," she finally said between bites.

"Speaking of…" John rose, a huge smile spreading across his face as a tall good-looking man strolled over to the table. "Hey, Mac, how's it going?"

"Thought that was you, J.T." Grinning broadly, Mac,

who'd been a friend since grade school, clasped John's hand in one of his and slapped him on the back with the other. "But then I saw the lady and decided it couldn't possibly be. She's way too classy for the likes of you.

"Excuse me, ma'am," Mac continued, turning to Ali, all flirty smiles and engaging charm, "but didn't anyone warn you about this guy?"

"Okay, okay, knock it off," John cut in, enjoying his friend's good-natured ribbing. "I may live to regret this but, Ali, this back-stabbing, second-rate busboy is Brett McDonald, the owner of this greasy spoon. Mac—Alison Samuels. And that's *Dr.* Samuels to you."

Mac arched a brow. "A doctor, huh?"

"Veterinarian," Ali clarified, grinning over their antics and obvious affection.

"Just so I have this straight, you came with him willingly?" Mac asked in aside.

"Sit down and quit trying to beat my time. The lady knows what she wants."

"And right now, it's to compliment the chef," Ali said, grinning between them. "This is absolute heaven."

"I give foot rubs, too, if you get tired of the cowboy." Mac winked then turned to John. "So, how's it going, bud? Long time, no see, and all that."

John lifted his wine, drank. "I'm good. Don't have to ask how you are," he added looking around the crowded restaurant. "Cha-ching."

Mac grinned—a quick dazzling flash of white teeth

set in a face that drew women like honey drew flies. "Yeah. Can't complain. Business has been great."

"Understandable," Ali said. "Not only is the food fabulous, the entire concept is smart and clever. I mean—naming the restaurant Spaghetti Western? It's genius."

"You," Mac said, flashing his grin at Ali, "are clearly a woman of great intellect and wit—which begs me to repeat my question—you came with this guy willingly?"

"Obviously, you two have issues," Ali said laughing. "I'll just make myself scarce for a minute or two so you can work them out."

After patting her mouth with her napkin, she picked up her purse and headed for the ladies' room.

"Hit the mother lode on that one, pal," Mac said, appreciation in his eyes as he watched her walk away from the table. "Someone slap you up alongside your head and knock some sense into you or what?"

Or what, John thought and promptly changed the subject to something he had a handle on—like an argument over their favorite football teams and how the preseason was shaping up.

He wasn't about to discuss Ali but he couldn't agree with Mac more. He'd definitely hit the mother lode. Now the question was, how aggressively was he going to mine it.

This is what he'd wanted from the beginning. A good time with a beautiful woman. And this woman was the embodiment of his ideal. She was independent and self-contained. A woman who wouldn't feel the need to fix him or get too deeply involved because she had her own need for distance. It wasn't always that way. That's why the minute a woman showed signs of wanting more from him than physical intimacy, he was gone. If they started telling him their life stories, well, then they'd expect the same from him and that just wasn't going to happen.

That was part of why the doc was so appealing. Her secrecy came with a built-in guarantee she would respect his secrets. As warm as she was, she remained guarded and distant. And sad. That part still messed him up a little and made him more determined than ever to put a smile on her face.

As she came back to the table and sat down, looking like the lead in one of his most erotic fantasies, he told himself he'd show her a good time, treat her right, and, if he sensed she'd started wanting more, he'd do everything in his power to make sure they parted as friends.

Right now, all she wanted was to use him to open herself up to living in life. No problem. She could use him up.

She smiled at him across the table. Yeah. She knew exactly what he was good for. And it didn't suddenly bother him that she might not want or expect a little more. It didn't bother him a bit.

Just like this niggling sense of discomfort that had settled in the pit of his belly had nothing to do with disappointment that he could never be the kind of man a woman like her deserved to have in her life long term.

"X-Men," John said decisively when Ali asked him to name his favorite movie. "The first one."

"Figures," Ali said. "It's definitely a tech-head movie."

They were sitting on her front porch swing again, rocking slowly back and forth, listening to the night sounds and a country ballad drifting down the street from someone's radio and playing twenty questions. On the way back to Sundown from Spaghetti Western, they'd gone through favorite books, songs, artists. Trivial things, keeping it light, nothing too personal. Now they were down to movies.

"Am I supposed to feel insulted or complimented by that tech-head remark?" John asked with a playful gleam in his eye. "Never mind. If I had to ask it *definitely* wasn't a compliment. It's that pocket protector image I planted in your mind, isn't it? You've been picturing me with black horn rims, white socks and high-water pants ever since."

Ali laughed, enjoying their silly banter as she hadn't enjoyed a conversation for a very long time. And pocket protectors were the furthest thing from her mind. So were tight blue jeans. When he'd shown up for their date tonight wearing dark summer-weight dress pants and a pale blue button-down shirt, she'd been thinking he could adapt to whatever the environment called for—

and look great. There was a raw sexuality about this man in tight jeans and a Resistol, a polished sensuality about the same man tonight.

His dark eyes were filled with humor as he sat beside her, waiting for her response.

"Actually, my first impression has pretty well stuck."

He'd been on horseback the first time she'd seen him. She'd been answering a call for a vet. A yearling filly had gone colicky on him and he'd been astride a big bay gelding leading the filly around an outdoor corral. Keeping the yearling from going down had been crucial until Ali had been able to get there. Her breath had actually caught at the picture he'd made—rugged masculinity, youthful confidence and one of the most perfectly sculpted faces she'd ever seen.

"The first time I saw you is pretty well burned in my brain, too."

She pushed out a laugh. "There's a pleasant thought. I'd just come from a marathon calf vaccination session at Lou Bradford's. I not only smelled like manure, if I remember right, I was wearing some of it."

"You looked incredible. Your hair was tucked up underneath a ball cap…little strands trailing down the back of your neck."

His hand, which had been resting on the back of the swing, touched her there, demonstrating.

"Here," he said, his voice suddenly husky.

His fingers caressed with the softness of breath and sent a shiver eddying down her spine.

Ali made herself take a deep breath, inhaling the cool mountain night, the sweet fragrance of honeysuckle twining around her neighbor's porch, but most of all the scent of the man so close beside her.

Her heart beat like thunder as his fingers stroked and the swing slowly rocked and the world shrank to the few feet of night they shared.

"Is this going to happen tonight, Ali?" he whispered softly.

Is this going to happen?

That straightforward. That direct.

Is this going to happen?

She hadn't expected him to ask. She'd expected him to act. She ached with wanting for him to act. Every muscle in her body was clenched with expectation and anticipation and…oh, God.

The guilt came out of nowhere.

Crippling. Crushing.

She closed her eyes, felt the sting of tears.

The entire night had led up to intimacy. She'd known it. She'd dressed for it. She'd looked forward to it.

And now, she didn't know if she could go through with it.

He must have sensed her hesitancy.

The stroke of his fingers on her neck stopped. The motion of the porch swing stilled. She could feel his gaze on her in the dark. Waited for the anger. He deserved to be angry. So it was only their first official date. Neither one of them had had any doubts about where it had been headed. She'd been sending signals all night, letting him know she was ready to cross one of those lines she'd drawn for herself.

And now, she was backing away.

Beside her, he let out a deep breath.

"It's okay," she heard him say and felt the gentle rocking motion of the swing again.

He pulled her against him. Pressed her head against his shoulder and held her while a silent tear streamed down her cheek. She felt like the biggest coward and the biggest fool in the world.

"I'm sorry," she whispered. "I...wow. I thought..."

When she trailed off, he picked up the thought for her.

"You thought you were ready and you're not." His tender acceptance brought new tears. "It's okay," he repeated, rubbing his hand up and down her bare arm.

To her surprise, she realized she was shivering.

"Well, hey—dinner was great, huh?" He squeezed her arm affectionately.

She pushed out a dismal laugh, then pulled away from his comforting hold to find her purse and dig around inside for a tissue. "This is so embarrassing."

"No cause." He touched a hand to her hair. "I had a great night."

She wiped her nose then managed a feeble smile. "I did, too. In fact, I had a fantastic time."

He firmed his lips, nodded. "Well, I'd best be moseying on back to the bunk house. There's a cold shower waiting with my name on it."

She laughed, as he'd intended her to. "Who are you, John Tyler? Computer nerd, man about town or aw-shucks cowpoke?"

He stood, reached for her hands and drew her to her feet with him. "I'm the man who's gonna hang around until you're ready," he said, his dark eyes searching her face.

She wasn't sure what he saw—other than a red nose and running mascara. But he didn't see a fool. At least his eyes said he didn't even though that's exactly what she felt like.

He pulled her close, wrapped her tight then pressed a kiss to the top of her head. "Get some sleep."

This is me. Nothing complicated, he'd said last night.

She disagreed. He was far more complex than either one of them had given them credit for. That sudden knowledge made her brave. And decisive.

"John." She stopped him with a hand on his arm.

His gaze probed hers in the dark.

"Ask me again," she whispered and felt her heart pounding, pounding, pounding in her breast.

He turned to fully face her, those deep brown eyes searching hers.

"Better yet…don't ask." She shivered when his hand came up, cupped her jaw.

She saw the moment it registered in his eyes. A wisp of smoke, then the flare of fire. Spontaneous, instant. Hot.

He understood what she needed from him—how necessary it was that he take control. He understood that she ached for that powerful rush of lust and desire, how she needed to be swept off her feet by a man who was a little wild, a little rough around the edges, a man who would take the choice away from her. A man who would take her by storm, a man who would be forceful so she could blame him and not herself if she got hurt when she took the fall.

This man was all of those things. Wild and beautiful. Impulsive.

A risk.

"Tell me what you want, Ali."

His hoarse whisper caressed her nerve endings like a lover's hand, rough and needy, demanding that she tell him what he already knew.

"You know what I want."

His hand slid across her throat to the back of her neck and burrowed into her hair. Slowly, deliberately, he wrapped it around his fingers and used it to pull her flush against him. "Say it."

She swallowed around the lump of excitement clogging her throat, so aroused by his gruff demand her knees almost buckled.

"Say it," he repeated, tightening his grip in her hair and lowering his head.

When he pressed his open mouth against her throat, the words escaped on a breathless plea. "Take me."

Eight

Consumed. There was no other way to describe it. She felt consumed by him. Thrilled by him as he growled low in his throat, aligned his mouth with hers and kissed her like he intended to devour her in huge, greedy bites.

He wasn't subtle about what he wanted as he cupped her jaw in his hand and nudged her mouth open for the invasion of his tongue…and the consumption began in earnest.

She'd never been kissed like this. Like she was water and he was dying of thirst. Like she was sun and after years of darkness he'd just found his way into the light. It was earthy and raw and so arousing she didn't know if her breath caught because of the shock or the pleasure. There was so much of both. And she needed it. Needed it as badly as he appeared to need her.

"Inside," he murmured, lifting his head long enough to get a bead on their location before he covered her mouth again and walked her backward toward the door.

Once they reached it, he backed her up against it, bracketed her face with both hands and dipped inside her mouth for another deep, carnal kiss. This time her knees did buckle and if all of him hadn't been pressed up against all of her, she would have slithered into a puddle on the porch floor.

"Open it," he ordered, scooping her up in his arms.

Somehow, she managed the door handle. Somehow, they made it inside. And somehow, sometime in the midst of his commanding seduction, she was no longer uncertain. No longer unsure.

She wanted to make love with this man. This man who carried her up the stairs, then stopped halfway up to lean against the banister and kiss her until her head was swimming. His need was huge. But his innate gentleness—a trait he'd shown her time and again with his animals and with her when she'd repeatedly sent him away—would never allow him to hurt her. This she knew without qualifiers. And she welcomed his aggressive seduction without fear.

No, he would never hurt her—her bedroom door, however, didn't fare so well. When he found it closed, he kicked it open. She was aware of the sound of wood hitting wood, but just barely because he was kissing her again and the blood was rushing through her ears like a freight train blocking out everything but his nearness and her need.

His lips were incredible. A delicious blend of soft mobility and dangerous hunger. She savored the taste of him, the greed in him, and felt a surge of power so strong and sweet it made her smile against his lips when she sucked his tongue farther into her mouth and gently stroked it with her own.

"Off," he said on a throaty groan and let her go long enough to set her on her feet by the bed.

He sat down on the edge of the mattress, his gaze never leaving hers and started unbuttoning his shirt. When she simply stood in front of him, relishing each inch of skin revealed as he jerked the shirt off his shoulders and shrugged out of it, he glared at her through smoldering eyes.

"Off," he repeated, gruffer this time. Impatient.

A surge of joy burst through her, so strong, so instantaneous, she couldn't stop herself. She laughed. At her power over him. At his power over her.

When his eyes darkened like storm clouds, she laughed again.

"You Tarzan, me Jane?" she ventured, amused, in spite of herself over his monosyllabic orders.

"Hey…you started this," he reminded her and reached for her, drawing her close until she stood between his open thighs.

"Then why don't you finish it, cowboy?" Feeling

brazen and bold, she sagged against him in wanton invitation.

"Oh, I intend to. With pleasure," he whispered. "But just remember. You had your chance to take this off yourself."

"Is that a threat, Mr. Tyler?"

"You bet your sweet ass, Doctor." Watching her face, he cupped the back of her thighs with his big, workingman's hands and with a slow, tantalizing glide, worked his way upward. "Sweet, sweet ass," he repeated, cupping her cheeks, caressing her through black satin, then skimming up and under her panties to massage bare skin.

"Umm…a—"

"No talking," he said. "Just experience. I want you to feel this. Just feel it," he repeated, his voice deep and low as he slowly drew her panties over her hips and down her thighs, caressing her every inch of the way. He steadied her with a hand on her hip when he told her to step out of them.

"Leave the heels on. We'll deal with them later. Right now, I want them right where they are."

Desire shot through her belly like an arrow when he unhooked her panties from around her ankle, scrunched them in his hand and with his eyes locked on hers, brought them to his face and inhaled.

It was shocking. It was thrilling. And it made her so warm and achy between her thighs, she felt light-headed and impatient and vulnerable all at once.

"John—"

"Shhh." He pressed his face against her, just below her breasts, nuzzled her sweetly while his hands started something that would never be classified as sweet.

She sucked in her breath on a serrated sigh, braced herself with her hands on his shoulders as he caressed her bottom with one hand and with the other, found the most vulnerable part of her.

"Don't…move," he ordered, stroking her where she was wet and swollen and so wonderfully sensitive she couldn't suppress a groan.

"Don't move," he repeated when her hips bucked involuntarily against his hand.

She closed her eyes, tried to do what he said but…oh…oh…he was relentless as he probed and caressed and drove her to a level of sensation that brought tears to her eyes, had her digging her fingers into the tense muscle of his shoulders.

It was so good. It was so incredibly good. Too good. Too much. Too soon. She was going to lose it if he didn't stop. And she wanted him with her when she went over the edge.

Frantic for relief, she circled his wrist with her hand. "Please. No more."

Heart hammering, she met his eyes. Saw the satisfaction there and understood that he knew exactly what he was doing to her. He was driving her wild. Finessing her to a fever pitch with the skillful stroke of his fingers and the heated look in his eyes.

Without a word, he withdrew his hand. The ache the

absence of his touch left behind was almost painful. But then he was touching her again. His fingers lightly skimming up her bare arms, hooking under the spaghetti straps of her dress and deliberately waiting for her reaction.

It came with a shivering sigh. "Please."

His gaze burned into hers. "Take off your bra. The first time I see you out of this dress, I want to see nothing but bare skin."

She was past being shocked. But not past the instantaneous sensual reaction. Heat speared to the tips of her breasts, then drizzled like hot wax to the core of her that was already missing his touch, waiting and wanting it again.

With unsteady hands, she reached up beneath the low-cut bodice of her dress. With trembling fingers, she unhooked the clasp between her breasts, felt the weight of them fall free as she drew out the black strapless bra that matched her panties. A muscle in his jaw worked. The breadth of his chest expanded as he drew in a controlled breath.

Then ever so slowly, he started tugging on the straps. The dress was a silky crepe and it slid smoothly down her skin before catching on her erect nipples and creating an amazing, erotic friction when he intentionally rubbed the fabric back and forth across them.

"You are a wicked, wicked man," she murmured as his action intensified her need and edged her back to that place where sensation and desire not only drove her, they devoured her.

"I'm a man who's wild for you," he whispered, his breath ragged when he finally tugged the dress all the way to her waist then watched it slide in a pool of black to the floor around her feet.

The touch of his fingers on her sensitive breasts made her shiver. The gentle exploration as he tested the weight of her, the shape of her and, finally, the extent of her arousal forced a quivering breath when he brushed his thumbs over her nipples.

With a deliberate languor that drove her to yet another level of sensation, he moved his hands to her back, spread his fingers wide just under her shoulder blades and urged her closer to his mouth.

She'd never felt more vulnerable...or more aroused as she stood before him in nothing but her four-inch heels and her forty-year-old body. He didn't seem to mind. In fact, he didn't seem to mind at all. The low growl as he took her nipple in his mouth and drew her in said he loved her body. The slow, cherishing glide of his hands on her back, circling her waist, cupping her hips then lifting her, spreading her thighs until her knees were digging into the bed on either side of his hips and she was straddling him, said he adored her body.

And she adored what he was doing to her. His mouth was warm. His tongue a masterful tease as he flicked it over her nipple then laved her areola with liquid strokes and silken glides.

She cradled his head in her hands, pressed herself into his mouth and with the confidence of a desirable woman let him do whatever he would do to her. And, oh, was he an inventive lover.

She didn't know when she'd ended up on her back. Was mistily aware of him rolling away, tugging off his boots then the rest of his clothes.

When the light on her bedside table flicked on, shedding a soft glow over the bed and exposing what the darkness had hidden, she had a moment of trepidation. Until she saw his eyes. And read the appreciation there.

"You are amazing," he said, standing over her, one knee on the bed, digging into the mattress at her hip.

"Look who's talking," she said, feeling a power so great she boldly reached for him, stroked a finger down the length of his thigh. He was as beautiful below the waist as he was above. Muscle and sinew. Power and strength.

And from the size of his very impressive erection, he was extremely happy to be with her this way.

One corner of his mouth turned up in a sexy, slumberous grin as he twisted at the hip, snagged his pants from the floor and fished a condom out of his pocket.

"For the lady," he said handing her the packet then crawling onto the bed and kneeling over her on all fours. "Take your time," he murmured, nudging her arms out of the way and lowering himself so he could nuzzle at her bare breasts again. "I know I plan to."

A man of his word, this one. By the time he was done kissing her, and licking her and nibbling her breasts, the inside of her thighs, the arch of her foot as he slowly removed her heels then tossed them over his shoulder, she felt like she'd aged a decade. And somewhere along the way her bones had disappeared. She was as limp as overcooked pasta and couldn't have been happier for it.

He lifted the condom from her fingers. "Guess that's going to be my job, after all," he said with a smile of a man who knew he'd decimated a woman with pleasure and was damn proud of his handiwork.

She sucked in her breath on a gasp as he eased himself inside of her…hard and heavy and thick, and what couldn't possibly get any better did. Stroke by stroke he took her higher, thrust by thrust he drove her wilder until pleasure spiraled in a blurry maze of electric blues and fiery reds and the world was reduced to this time, this place, this man who made her remember what it was like to be a woman yet stole her capacity to recall her own name.

Lying on his side beside her, John propped himself up on an elbow, slowly recovering from some of the most incredible sex of his life. Maybe *the* most incredible sex of his life.

He'd known they'd be compatible in bed. He'd known he could give her pleasure. What he hadn't known was the extent of the contentment he'd feel in the giving.

She'd been so incredibly responsive. So wildly sensual. He'd loved her stunning vulnerability…and her total lack of inhibition when she'd finally let go.

Her body was amazing. He loved the soft resiliency of her hips. The pillowy fullness of her breasts. And he'd been right about her skin. From that sweet spot just under the curve of her jaw, to the even sweeter spot inside her thighs, she was as silky as a summer breeze.

And he wanted her again.

"Are you asleep?" he whispered, then because he couldn't stop himself, he leaned down and pressed a kiss on her bare shoulder.

A long, deep breath confirmed that she'd heard him. On another deep breath, she lifted her arms, then let them drop, limp and listless above her head. "Closer to comatose. Thank you for that."

He smiled against her shoulder, nipped her lightly as she lay on her back, the sheet tangled low on her hip, her breasts bare and beautiful in the soft light.

"The pleasure was definitely mine. Next time you want to be taken, I'm your man," he teased, reminding her of the words that had propelled them from her porch to a tangle of sheets.

"You really think there'll be a next time?" Her lips twitched as she opened her eyes and grinned up at him. "Now that we got it out of our systems, don't you think we can just go on about our business?"

Fat chance.

"So you think this was just a one-night stand, do you?"

She reached up and brushed the hair out of his eyes. "Well…maybe we can go for two."

Laughing, he rolled to his back and dragged her on

top of him. "Fifty bucks says I can parlay that number into multiple digits."

She smiled down into his eyes and it stunned him again just how beautiful she was. "Do your worst, cowboy."

"Oh, darlin', I plan to. I truly do plan to."

Watching her face, he ran his hands down her back, over her hips and all the way down to the back of her thighs. When he spread her legs until her knees were digging into the mattress at his hips and did a little exploring between them, her breath caught. Her heartbeat quickened against his. With the sinewy movements of a sleek, lazy cat, she braced her hands on his chest and pushed herself up until she sat astride him, her eyes closed in dreamy pleasure. And then she was moving against him, her beautiful breasts swaying to the most sensual, erotic rhythm…and he was the one catching his breath and frantically searching for another condom.

He left her before dawn. He left her sleeping. Not because he wanted to. Not because he experienced a disconcerting notion that if he didn't leave, and soon, he might have a hard time leaving at all.

He left because he never let himself spend the night in a woman's bed. The black hole sometimes opened up at night and he didn't want to suck her down into it with him.

Besides, it was best for her. Small town. Small minds. He didn't want anyone waking up in the morning and seeing his truck in front of her house, putting two and two together and making it hard for her.

It wasn't normally a long ride home from Sundown. Twenty miles, twenty minutes. But that was when he didn't slow down every mile or two and think real hard about doing a one-eighty and crawling back into her nice warm bed. Next to her nice warm body.

Heaven above, did he love her body.

And he loved making love with her.

Which was another reason why it had been a wise move to head on out of town. He didn't want to foster any false impressions. Didn't want her thinking this was anything more than two people who liked each other hooking up for some mind-blowing sex. Because that's all it was. Mutual attraction. Mutual satisfaction. Everybody parted as friends in the morning.

At least that's what he kept telling himself. He'd told her, too, before things had ever gotten to this point. He'd made it clear that he wanted her, but that he didn't do serious relationships.

But man, oh man, was she something.

He cupped his hand around the back of his neck, rolled his head and wondered what she'd think when she woke up and found him gone? Would she miss him? Would she appreciate that fact that he'd taken time to sneak out into her backyard and pluck one of the wild yellow roses growing up the trellis by the tool shed and lay it on the pillow by her head?

Would she smile at the note he'd left with it?

He dropped his hand, stared straight ahead, a little uncomfortable suddenly with the lengths he'd taken to make sure she knew he hadn't just skipped without a second thought about how she'd take it.

It was a first. He didn't leave notes. He didn't regret not spending the night. And, generally, he didn't start trying to figure out when he was going to be able to carve out some more free time to pick up where they'd left off.

As the day wore on, he started arguing with himself over whether or not he should call her yet that day.

One minute he'd be plotting reasons why he should, the next he'd be talking himself out of it. By midmorning, he had himself convinced he needed to cool his jets so she wouldn't get the wrong idea; by noon, he was contemplating his cell phone.

It was damn disgusting. And confusing as hell. He'd never reacted this way to a woman.

"Hell," he muttered and punched in her number as he strode out of the barn for the house to throw together a sandwich for lunch. He was making too big a deal out of it. The doc knew the score. And if she didn't, well, he'd set her straight when the time came.

But in the meantime, in the meantime, if he didn't see her again, he was going to bust a seam.

Ali sat on the back porch steps alternately sipping coffee and smelling the wilted yellow rose she'd found on her pillow when she'd awakened around nine. She listened to birdsong and the sound of the Wilson kids playing in the tiny plastic swimming pool in their back yard. And she wondered how it was that yesterday morning she'd awakened a mature, no-nonsense businesswoman but this morning when she'd opened her eyes she'd digressed into a baffling, thrilling, distressing mix of adolescent and over-the-hill octogenarian.

At least she moved like a senior citizen. Her body ached in places she hadn't known she had places, yet it was an ache that was undercut by a loose-limbed satisfaction she didn't ever remember feeling before. As for the adolescence part… Lord help her. Emotionally, she felt like she was flying high on her first schoolgirl crush. She felt giddy and scattered and as she drew the note John had left on her pillow out of her pocket and read it—*again*—she couldn't stop the smile from creeping over her face.

> This rose is yellow,
> sorry it's not edible.
> I'm a happy fellow,
> last night was *incredible.*
> Sorry about the rhyme,
> but I ran out of time…
> I'll call. Sleep in. J.T.

Smiling dreamily, she refused to acknowledge how many times she'd read his silly note, refused to consider why she'd carried it with her from room to room, propping it where she could see it, then finally pocketed it so it was with her every where she went.

Just like she refused to acknowledge that she smiled a little too much over it. And over her memories of last night.

John Tyler was an amazing lover. And talk about stamina. She had never known she was capable of multiple orgasms...multiple times. And she'd never done some of the things they had done last night.

Of course, she'd only had one other lover and that had been David. He'd been a gentle, intellectual soul with very little adventure or wildness in his nature. Their lovemaking had been wonderful and special and sweet. But sometimes, sometimes she had secretly wished that he'd been a little more spontaneous...a little more of a free spirit.

Her smile vanished when she realized that this was the first time she'd thought about David since last night. She waited for the crushing guilt, for the regret to settle on her shoulders and weigh down her buoyant mood.

But strangely, it didn't come. Neither did the feelings of regret over what she and John had shared last night. Instead, she felt a sort of peace with herself. She would always and forever miss David. She would always and forever mourn him. But as she sat there, with the Sunday sun beating down and a soft breeze dancing on the air, she felt too good about life to bash herself over the head because she'd finally taken the plunge and dived back into it. Instead of standing by the side of the pool, worrying about sinking, she was swimming again. And it felt good.

She would always grieve over David. But now that

she had taken this huge step and landed back among the living, she would no longer confuse her grief with guilt.

She had nothing to feel guilty about.

And today, she had a lot to be happy about.

She had a wonderful lover whom she liked and enjoyed and who wanted the same thing she did. A little pleasure along the way. Nothing more.

Feeling a lightheartedness she hadn't felt in way too long, she stood to go back inside and tackle the final coat of paint in the living room.

When the phone rang just as she opened the screen door, she didn't even try to quell her excitement. A lover's intuition told her it was John.

"Hello."

"Hello, Doc. How's every little thing?"

She leaned against the wall, a sappy smile splitting her face. "Why, every little thing is just fine and dandy, thank you very much."

He chuckled, all sexy and low and suggestive. "Glad to hear it. I was worried that I might have been a little too…greedy last night."

"Greed," she said, loving the husky resonance in his voice that told her he felt as satisfied and yet as insatiable as she did, "often gets a bad rap."

"Amen to that. Did you find my note?"

"I did. Thank you."

"Shakespeare, I'm not."

"But you are so many other things. And it's the thought that counts."

"I'm having some thoughts right now. Wanna hear them?"

She laughed. "Not if I want to get anything done today." Lord. Listen to her. She was flirting on the phone.

He was quiet for a moment and when he finally spoke again, the need in his voice sent a firestorm of arousal skittering through her blood. "When can I see you again?"

A dizzying rush of desire weakened her knees. "Tonight?"

"God, yes. Come out to the ranch. I'll be waiting for you."

Nine

John had just stepped out of the shower and thrown on clean jeans and a T-shirt when he heard a car pull up in the drive. *Finally.* It was late, going on eight. There hadn't been too much sleeping going on last night in Ali's bed and he'd pushed himself hard all day, buzzed on anticipation. A couple of hours ago, he'd let down, tired to the bone. When he walked outside into a twilight tinged with apricot and lavender and plenty of lingering July heat, and saw Ali getting out of her car, though, suddenly he wasn't tired any more.

He stood on his front stoop, arms crossed over his chest as she opened her car door and stepped out into the gathering dusk.

Now there, he realized, was a sight that would be tattooed on his memory for a very long time. Mountain met sky in purple relief behind her. The sun, about to dip low on the horizon, set fire to her hair and limned her in a golden glow.

She wore a pair of yellow shorts and a white tank top. And as she walked closer, a tentative smile on her face, he could see she'd applied a touch of lip gloss. He couldn't wait to lick it off of her.

As a matter of fact, it took every ounce of his willpower not to haul her up and over his shoulder and deposit her on the nearest horizontal surface.

"You're looking pretty foxy tonight there, Doc," he said instead, looking his fill and liking it, drawing out the anticipation to make their lovemaking that much sweeter. "And pretty sure of yourself," he suddenly realized, judging by the look on her face.

"Well, I'm a woman on a mission."

"I'm going to go out on a limb here and say I like the sound of that." Like maybe her mission was making love to him until *he* was comatose this time.

"We'll know soon enough. Come help me."

He followed her back to her car, enjoying the sassy sway of her hips and the way her hair bounced against her back with every step.

"I thought maybe you could use a refill," she said, reaching inside the car then handing him a gallon-sized plastic bag full of oatmeal-raisin cookies.

"Hey." Something warm and mellow filled his chest.

"This is great. I'm going to have to figure out a way to repay you for these. Let me think." He raked her body with a long, thorough sweep of his eyes. "Oh, wait, I've got it."

She laughed, a husky, throaty sound. "I'll just bet you do. First, though, I took a chance that you hadn't eaten and brought dinner. I figured if you had, you could always warm it up tomorrow."

"You brought me dinner?" Another warm fuzzy feeling settled in his chest. It wasn't the first time a woman had brought him dinner. Hell, women tended to want to do a lot of things for him. They'd cooked, they'd cleaned, they'd washed his clothes in bids to settle him down and show him what good marriage material they'd make. It had always made him nervous. It had always made him walk.

Tonight, it simply made him smile.

"Don't get too excited. It's carryout from the Dusk to Dawn. Nadine said hi, by the way."

Nadine and her husband Chet Haskins had owned the Dusk for as long as John could remember. And they knew everybody's business.

"Are there any secrets in this town?" she asked with a rueful smile.

"Not so anyone would notice. Hey…are you up for a little adventure?" he asked as a sudden idea struck him.

She raised a brow. "What kind of adventure?"

"A twilight picnic."

"Sounds wonderful."

He kissed her lightly. "Let me grab a blanket. We'll take my truck."

The little pocket lake that lay in the belly of a green canyon on the west end of his ranch had always been one of John's favorite places. And as they drove over the last hill leading to a shoreline dotted with aspens and pines and blanketed with pasture grass that was resting for the fall grazing season, he could see that Ali was taken with it, too.

"It's like a postcard," she said after he cut the motor. Then she simply sat, taking in the lush, verdant beauty of the valley, the gently rolling foothills and the towering trees climbing the slopes toward the mountain range beyond.

"Thought you'd like it." He opened the door and climbed out. "You bring the grub—I've got the blanket."

It would be dark soon, so along with the blanket, he'd grabbed a camping lantern so they'd have some light to guide them back to the truck later. Much later if he had his way.

He led her down to the lakeshore then got busy spreading out the blanket. When he'd finished, he looked up and found her toeing off her sandals.

"It's just too good to pass up," she said, smiling up at him.

"So is this," he said, unable to hold back any longer.

He drew her into his arms and kissed her. "Hello," he whispered against her mouth.

"Hello." Dewy soft eyes looked into his from beneath lashes that he'd never noticed were so long and lush.

He kissed her again, slow and deep. "I'm glad you're here."

She looped her arms around his neck and rose up on her tiptoes to get closer. "So am I."

For long, leisurely moments they just stood that way. Snuggled close and kissing. He didn't think he'd ever get tired of kissing her.

"This is nice," he said and drawing her closer trailed kisses across her face, along the sweet line of her jaw, then worked his way back to her mouth again.

She sighed in contentment. "Very, very nice."

"I know a way to make it even nicer." He drew back far enough so that he could see her face. "How do you feel about skinny-dipping?"

"I…um…what?"

He laughed. "Let's go for a swim."

She looked at the lake, then back at him, working hard not to look horrified, and failing miserably. "In there?"

"Of course in there."

"But…aren't there fish and *things* in there?

"Believe me, darlin', they are little fish and little things and they're a lot more worried about you than you could ever be about them."

Clearly, she wasn't convinced as he let her go, tugged his T-shirt out of his jeans and whipped it over his head. After tossing his shirt behind him on the blanket, he went to work on his boots.

"You're really going in there?" she asked, then did a little wide-eyed ogling when he undid his belt and shucked his jeans. "Oh…well…wow. You're not wearing underwear."

"Plannin' ahead, darlin'. Just plannin' ahead.

"So," he added, feeling himself grow hard as her gaze swept him from head to toe, then back to the rising proof of the effect she had on him. "You coming in?"

She blinked from him to the water. "Is it cold?"

"I sure do hope so. It's still as hot as blazes tonight."

And with that, he waded to the edge of the bank and made a shallow surface dive. He emerged ten yards from shore. Whipping his wet hair from his eyes, he treaded water and grinned back at her.

"Come on, Doc. It feels great."

Her pinched frown told him she wasn't so sure about this. She looked over her shoulder, then back at him. "We won't… I mean…Clive or someone won't find us out here, right?"

"Doc, darlin', there's not another human soul within twenty miles of here. Now, quit stalling. It's getting lonely out here."

With one final look back toward the car, she drew a bracing breath and slowly lifted her tank top up and over her head. Her shorts came next and then she was standing there in nothing but panties and bra.

His mouth went dry. Someday, he was going to have to have her model her entire collection of underwear for him. He loved the black satin she'd worn last night. He was wild about the peach-colored bits of lace that almost covered the important parts right now.

But right now, all he wanted was skin.

"Scaredy-cat," he taunted. "City slicker."

"All right. All right, you don't have to resort to name-calling." She was grinning as she reached behind her back to unhook her bra. "But so help me, if I get bit by a fish or a snake or something, you'd better have the name of a good lawyer."

He was grinning, too…until she tossed her bra on the blanket beside his T-shirt. And then he was just plain staring and loving everything he saw. She had the most incredible breasts. Heavy and creamy with dusky brown nipples set in the middle of the prettiest pink areolas. And right now, they were diamond-hard. So was he by the time she'd shimmied out of her French-cut panties and stood before him in all her naked glory.

"You are absolutely beautiful," he said, hearing the awe in his voice, feeling the rapid beat of his blood rushing to his groin.

Beautiful and proud of her body as she pulled back her shoulders, drew a fortifying breath and walked into the lake.

"Oh, my God. It's f-freezing."

"You'll get used to it."

"N-not in this lifetime."

The water had just reached her knees when he realized he couldn't wait to meet her halfway. He had to get his hands on her. Now.

"Then we'll just have to figure out a way to warm you up."

He found bottom, then started walking toward her, meeting her just as the water was lapping at her navel. She looked like a sea nymph standing there, her hair curling over her shoulder, her eyes beckoning and bright.

And he couldn't stop himself. He reached for her, went down on his knees and drew one beautiful breast into his mouth. Then he gorged himself on the silk-and-velvet texture of her while she laced her fingers through his hair and offered herself up for his pleasure.

He'd never received so much in the giving. Never realized how good it could feel when a woman literally turned boneless in his arms. He lifted his head, coaxed her wrists around his neck and drew her back into deeper water with him.

"Are you warm yet?"

"Getting there," she said dreamily, then abruptly screamed and damned near drowned him in a mad scramble to scale his body.

"What…Doc…what's wrong?"

"S-snake!" she gasped, burying her face against his throat. "It…it brushed against my thigh.

"It's not funny," she said when he broke into a grin, then an all-out chuckle.

"Stop laughing!" With a combination of terror and testiness, she slugged him on the shoulder. "I'm telling you there's a snake down there."

"Believe me, sweetie, that was no snake."

"Well, whatever it was, it was huge!"

"Why, thank you, darlin'," he said, then watched her face transition from horror to embarrassment when it finally dawned on her what had really been brushing up against her thigh.

She let out a breath of pure relief. Then a devilish gleam filled her eyes. "Well, now that I think about it, it wasn't all *that* big. In fact…it was just a teensy weensy little thing."

He loved this playful side of her. "Is that a fact?"

"Microscopic," she reiterated, fluttering her lashes.

"Doc?"

"Hmm?"

"Plug your nose." Then he dunked her.

"It's guys who don't kiss and tell," Peg pointed out over lunch Monday. "Women are expected to share every big, little and in-between detail. Now give it up."

Ali unwrapped her sandwich and popped open a can of lemonade. "We went to dinner. It was nice. Not too many details," she said evasively.

As much as she trusted Peg, she wasn't ready to talk about what was happening between her and John. It was new and exciting and hers. A love affair. It sounded so Victorian and yet it felt outrageous and bold and incredibly brazen.

And let's face it, she thought, feeling her cheeks flush red, making love in a mountain lake and then out in the open on a blanket under the stars *was* outrageous and bold and incredibly brazen. And wonderful.

"Okay, see, that's what I'm talking about," Peg said with a sage nod. "That rosy glow. That secret little smile."

Ali shrugged. "Sorry. Don't know what you're talking about."

"I'm talking about the fact that Homer Clayborne told Edith Snelling who told Max Winwood who told me that when Homer got up in the middle of the night Saturday to let his dog out, he just happened to see a certain rancher's pickup parked in front of your house."

Ali bit off a bite of her sandwich, took her time chewing and finally swallowed. "Mr. Clayborne is eighty years old and has cataracts. I don't think I'd be counting on anything he says he sees as gospel."

Peg studied her across the small table in the clinic waiting room. "So, it was that good, was it?"

Ali let out a long, contented sigh and gave it up. "Yeah. It was that good."

"I knew it! I knew you two were perfect for each other."

"Whoa, whoa, whoa. We are not a 'you two.' Don't go pairing us up as a couple. Don't make this into a relationship, because it's not. It's not," she insisted when Peg cut her a look. "At least not the kind you might want it to be."

"Then what kind of relationship is it?"

"The kind where two single adults are simply enjoying each other's company."

Peg would have kept after her forever, but fortunately,

Ali got a call and had to head out to the Crawfords', so she was able to dodge a second round of questions.

She liked John. She liked him a lot. He was fun and funny and sweet and so sexy she got all achy just thinking about being with him. But, like her, John knew his limits. As he said, he was just out for a good time. Nothing complicated. She had to respect that. And she had to remember that it was a combination of good chemistry and timing that had brought them together. Another place, another time when she hadn't felt so vulnerable or so lonely, she would never have considered getting involved with him.

She pulled into the Crawfords' lane reminding herself that she knew what love was. Love was what she'd felt for David. Sure, she felt some of those things for John, but not on that commit-forever level. And even if she did, by some stretch of the imagination, think that some of what she was feeling for John tapped the same vein as the feelings she'd had for David, it would pass. The newness of the affair, the excitement of the sex…well, it would wear off. And when it did, when it was no longer as compelling or as thrilling, one of them would end it.

And that would be the end of the story.

For now, she was going to enjoy it. She was going to live *in* life as John had suggested, not outside of it.

For the next two weeks, she definitely lived it large. John took her back to Spaghetti Western for dinner, took her to a movie where they shared popcorn and

Dots and no matter how many protests she whispered and how many times she tried to stop him, he managed to get in a little necking in the back row of the theater that reduced her to giggling like a schoolgirl. One blissfully gorgeous Sunday afternoon, he took her horseback riding in the foothills, pairing her up with Taco, a gentle buckskin mare.

Some nights they would sit on her front porch and swing in the dark and listen to music. Other nights they would go for sunset strolls. But always, always, they would make the most beautiful love. Love that left her breathless, love that left her boneless, love that left her vulnerable to emotions that if she didn't know better, and wasn't careful, could start to feel a whole lot like the real thing. A whole lot like love.

As the hot days and sultry summer nights passed, John was feeling pretty good about the arrangement with Ali. He'd never met a woman quite like her. Peg Reno and Ellie Savage had come close. He'd always had special feelings for them but Cutter and Lee were the perfect matches for those two strong women. They needed commitment.

Ali didn't. Like him, she was very careful to avoid any in-depth discussions about their pasts. They had plenty of other things to talk about and when they weren't talking, well, they found even more pleasurable ways to pass the time.

Everything was peachy. Everything was fine. Even

the nightmares had let up. And he hadn't had a flashback in weeks. Life was good. He had a lover he liked and respected, who was his intellectual equal, was exciting and giving in bed, and was content with their unspoken agreement to maintain a no-strings, no-strain relationship. And just because he found it harder and harder and harder to leave her bed at night, that didn't mean he was looking for something more.

Everyone else was, though. It was never more evident than when J.T. pulled up in front of the Dusk to Dawn around seven Wednesday night.

Whistling under his breath, he breezed into the restaurant and headed for the bar.

"Hey, J.T. What can I get you today?" Nadine Haskin asked with a grin big enough to match her gray-streaked hair when he sat down at the bar.

"We can start with a beer." He glanced at the chalkboard where the cook's choice changed daily. "And the special. Make it two. To go."

Most people would have retired by now, but not the Haskins. They liked what they did, liked the people and, like Sundown, not much in their lives changed.

"So, how're things in your world these days?" she asked, setting a shell of draft beer on the bar in front of him.

The question was as loaded as the shotgun he kept in the barn to chase off coyotes. And that was something that would never change, either. Folks knowing other folks' business.

"Right as rain," he answered evasively.

Nadine made a big show of wiping off the bar with a damp cloth that smelled of soap and chlorine bleach. "So what do you think of the new vet?"

He'd been waiting for *that* one. "Seems to know her business."

Nadine nodded sagely. "She sure is a little bit of a thing to be doing all that rough stock work."

"She can handle it," he said and stretched across the counter to grab the weekly newspaper the Haskins always kept for their clientele.

"Seen that firsthand, have you?"

"Yeah. Firsthand."

He buried his face in the paper—all ten pages of it— hoping Nadine might get the hint and drop the subject of Alison Samuels. No such luck.

"Seems like a nice enough sort. Pretty, too."

He grunted behind the paper.

"But then, you know that firsthand, too, don't cha?"

He let out a deep breath, slowly folded the paper. Smiled. "Don't forget my order now…and be sure you make it to go."

Damn busybody, John muttered under his breath five minutes later as he stowed the two dinners beside him in the front seat and headed for Ali's. Probably that wasn't fair. He liked Nadine. And she was just being human.

That didn't mean he had to like it when she poked her nose into his life. Didn't want her snooping around in Ali's life, either. Just like he didn't like people pairing him up with the doc. It wasn't like that between them and generally about the time he started hearing whispers of rumors of his name linked with a woman's, he knew it was time to move on. It made him feel cornered and uncomfortable.

With Ali, though, he was more concerned about how his reputation would affect hers. Like it or not, it could affect her business and that would be a sad turn of events.

He didn't want her hurt by this. And as he pulled up in front of her house, he was thinking that maybe he needed to let her know the buzz around town, give her a chance to bail if she wanted to.

As he walked up her front porch steps, he refused to acknowledge that the thought of her calling things off set a knot of anxiety coiling tight in his chest. Or that she'd become a habit it was going to be very hard to break.

"Ali?"

He rapped a knuckle on her front screen door. When she didn't answer, he walked on in. She was expecting him so he figured she wouldn't be far.

"Ali?" He called her name again as he walked through the foyer toward the kitchen—that's when he spotted the cookie on the floor at the bottom of the stairs leading to the second story.

"What the hell?"

He spotted another cookie on the first step and realized there was a trail of them leading all the way up the stairs.

Setting the take-out on the dining-room table, he

hooked his hat over a chair back and, grinning like a kid on Christmas morning, followed the trail to her open bedroom door.

And damn near swallowed his tongue.

There she was, buck naked on the bed but for three strategically placed cookies and a glad-to-see-him grin.

"Howdy, cowboy."

Ten

John leaned a shoulder against the door frame, felt a smile spreading like sunrise across his face and forgot completely about giving her a chance to bail before the gossip got out of control. "Well, hello. Don't you just look…sweet."

He bent down and picked up a cookie from the floor. Looked from it to her. "Special occasion?"

"Just wanted to make sure you didn't get lost."

"Not a chance," he said, walking across the bedroom, tugging his shirt out of his jeans. "I take it we're having dessert before dinner?"

"One of the things I appreciate most about you is that quick mind of yours. You don't miss a thing, do you?"

"Darlin'," he said, making quick work of the rest of his clothes, then easing down onto the bed beside her, "you can bet I'm not going to miss one single thing tonight. Starting here." He dipped his head to her breast and nudged the cookie aside with his nose.

He loved the sound she made when he touched her. A deep, throaty hum that was all honest reaction and brazen invitation. He loved that she was proud of her body and let him look his fill, and touch and explore until they were both so close to the edge desperation not only drove them, it consumed them.

But tonight, he wasn't going down easy. Tonight, he was going to take pleasure in the giving and so help him, he would draw out every sigh, every groan, every scream until she was completely and utterly devastated.

He knew now what took her there. Knew that sensitive and reactive spot at the very center of her nipple. Knew that she loved it when he flicked the pretty, pouty bead with his tongue then sucked her into his mouth hard and fast. And he used that knowledge to please her now, used his physical power to still her hands when she reached for him and urged him to hurry and come inside her.

"Not yet," he whispered, clasping her wrists in his hands and raising her arms above her head. With deliberate care, he positioned her fingers around the spokes in the brass headboard, stretched out full-length on top of her. "Hang on, little cowgirl. I'm going to take you for the ride of your life."

She blinked up at him through eyes gone misty with

pleasure, watched his face as he kissed his way down her body, lingering at her breasts, dipping deep into her navel before settling his shoulders between her thighs.

He looked up the length of her body, nuzzled soft springy curls and watched her eyes go dark.

"Sweet," he murmured, pressing a kiss to the inside of her left thigh. "Better and better," he drawled, finally finding and settling his mouth over that part of her that he found so fascinating and responsive and deliciously wet with anticipation and desire.

He burrowed deep and tasted heaven. Satin heat, silken and pink. He'd never seen anything so pretty. And he never tired of the way she opened like a vessel and invited him to drink his fill.

"J-John…"

His name escaped her lips on a keening sigh as he laved her with his tongue, tunneled his hands beneath her hips and tipped her to his mouth for better access. With each stroke he took her higher. With deep kisses and gentle suction, he drove her to the brink.

And then she was flying, her release liquid and convulsive, her breath labored and serrated as she let go of the headboard and reached for him, cradling his head in her hands and pressing his mouth against her to prolong the sensation.

Her entire body was trembling by the time he lifted his head. He was doing a little trembling, too, as he pressed a kiss on her damp curls. She was so beautiful…and so beautifully limp and languid.

He loved being responsible. He loved that when she opened her eyes drowsily, she had difficulty focusing. Loved that her voice was hoarse as she begged him to come inside her.

She didn't have to ask. She never had to ask. When they were in this bed he was hers and she was his and there was only one place he wanted to be. He entered her on a long, deep stroke.

Together they groaned, together they moved and when the warmth of her, the welcome of her, the unrelenting pleasure of sinking into her drew him back again and again and again, he finally took his own release. Electric. Devastating. Complete.

There was still a lot of daylight when John woke up. Ali was sleeping beside him as he carefully eased out of the bed…and spotted the picture on the top of her bureau.

He walked over, picked it up. He hadn't seen it before—but then, he'd never been in her bedroom in the daylight and the time they'd spent there had kept him and her well occupied with something other than checking out the décor.

The guy in the picture with Ali had his arms around her and she was leaning back against his chest, her hands covering his where they rested under her breasts. Brows knit, he studied the pose harder, and finally accepted he was seeing what he thought he was seeing.

He heard the sheets rustle on the bed behind him and turned with the picture still in his hand.

"My husband," she said, her gaze shifting from his face to the photograph.

She sat up slowly, gathering the sheet to her breast as she did, covering herself.

He couldn't think of anything to say. Couldn't think, period, because the blood had drained from his head. And he wasn't altogether sure why he felt like he'd just been gut shot.

"David," she continued, dragging the sheet with her and walking to his side. "I lost him. Four years ago. Cancer."

What? What did he say? What did he do? And what in the hell was he feeling? Sympathy, yes. But there was anger, too. And a sense of…hell. Loss. Like a huge gaping hole had just been carved out of his heart.

He stood like a stump as she took the picture from his hand and set it back on the bureau.

"I'm…sorry," finally came out. Clumsy. Hollow— which was exactly how he felt.

"Yeah," she said walking to the closet. She pulled out her robe and shrugged into it, knotting the belt at her waist. "Me, too.

"And right now, I'm hungry," she added, forcing a smile and a change of subject as she walked toward the bedroom door where she stopped and turned back to him. "Coming?"

"Yeah," he said absently. "Yeah. I'll be there in a minute."

But it was several minutes before he was able to pull

his fractured thoughts together enough to drag on his clothes. Several more before he could make himself walk down the stairs. His mood, like the sky, had transitioned to the gray shades of dusk. And she'd had a husband.

He hadn't intended to ask, but when he walked into the kitchen and saw her, the woman whose body he knew intimately but who, in actuality, he didn't know at all, he couldn't stop himself.

"Why did I not know you'd been married?"

"You never asked," she said simply.

No. He hadn't asked. He hadn't wanted to know about her past or her secrets or her sorrow. Now he did. And he wished he didn't. Because now he understood. Everything.

Her hesitancy at getting involved. The secrecy. The look that sometimes clouded her eyes but that she quickly hid when she realized he was watching her.

She was still living in the past…past life, past love, past pain. And if he didn't miss his guess, she was still in love with her husband. At least she thought she was or felt she should be.

Four years. It was a long time to hang on to something that was gone. And suddenly, he wished he were anywhere but here, where he was merely a substitute for the real thing.

His heart went haywire. He didn't have a clue why, but he felt cheated and lost and…empty. Hell, he was the one who'd set the ground rules. Knowing about her husband shouldn't change anything. In fact, it should make him a happy man. Right? No worries here that she might fall in love with him and want to get cozy.

So why did he feel like he'd been hit by a freight train?

Suddenly, he had to get out of there.

"You know, I think I'll pass on dinner," he said in a voice he knew betrayed his turmoil. "Fact is, I need to be heading back."

She didn't make noises about feeding him. She didn't ask if he wanted to talk. She just nodded, her blue eyes somber as she watched him turn and walk out the door.

Twenty minutes later, he was home. He walked straight to his bedroom and shut the door. Feeling like he'd just lost something vital. Something good. Something that might have been the very best thing that ever happened to him because he knew it was over between them.

Two weeks later, as Ali drove south out of Sundown toward the Tyler ranch, she still had a vivid picture in her mind of how John had looked when she'd told him about David. She hadn't understood it then. Hadn't understood why he'd seemed so angry. Why he'd run like the devil was on his tail. Neither did she understand why she'd just stood in silence and watched him go.

Now she did. Just like she understood why she hadn't seen him since. He hadn't been angry. He'd been devastated. He'd been hurt.

It was the last, the very last thing she'd expected from him. He was the heartbreaker, he was the good-time guy, the keep-it-simple, keep-it-loose playboy who didn't ever let his emotions get involved with his fun.

He was a fraud. He was involved. With her. As involved as she was with him, but everything in him was conditioned not to trust the truth. She knew why she'd had trouble recognizing what she was really feeling. She had no clue what haunted him.

Maybe she never would. But she had to at least try to make him see the truth.

Her hands were steady as she pulled into his drive with the express intent of telling him she was onto him. Telling him a whole lot more.

Talk about risks. When she got out of the car and spotted him working a yearling on a lunge line in the dry lot by the barn, she felt equal measures of relief and anxiety.

This was it. Gunfight at the not-so-okay corral.

Taking a deep breath, she walked toward him. She knew the moment he spotted her even though he made no sign of recognition or welcome. He continued turning a slow circle as he put the pretty chestnut filly through her paces.

"Looks like she's getting the hang of it," she said to break the icy silence even though the summer heat bore down.

His only response was a soft "Whoa, girl" as he reined the filly in.

His hat hid his face as he opened the gate, then led the chestnut through. After locking it behind him, he led the filly toward the pasture. Ali fell in step beside him.

"I've missed you."

"Been busy," he said, never breaking stride.

"Yeah. Me, too. We need to talk."

Still silent, he eased the filly through the pasture gate, unclipped the lead rope and gave her a slap on the rump so she'd know she was free to go about her business.

The yearling took off with a trumpeting snort and raced toward her pasture mates who were grazing on the slope of a hill.

The tranquility of the picture they made was in stark contrast to the riot of emotions roiling in her chest.

"I didn't tell you about David because I didn't want you to know," she said without preamble. "And because I felt I would be betraying his memory if I talked about him with you."

When he didn't say anything but didn't make any move to run, she went on. "We grew up together—next-door neighbors. Went together as early as grade school. He was my best friend. And I loved him."

He propped closed fists on his hips, stared hard at the grass at his feet—the ultimate picture of detachment. Yet she knew him now like she hadn't known him in the beginning. Only his tightly clenched jaw gave him away. He wasn't detached. He was heavily invested in what she was about to say whether he chose to acknowledge it or not.

"It was David's dream, not mine, that we set up a practice in the mountain west. And it was his dream that led me here.

"It was his dream," she added, hoping he was hearing, really hearing what she was about to say, "that led me to you."

That got a reaction. He looked at her, his eyes narrowed in what could be question, anger or pain.

"I didn't want this to happen. I didn't want to become involved with you. It felt like I was betraying David. It felt like I was letting go of the love I had for him."

A muscle in his jaw worked before he turned to go.

She stopped him with a hand on his arm. "Don't. Hear me out. I'm telling you this so you'll understand why it was so hard for me to make the decision to be with you. It didn't feel right to become involved with someone when I was still in love with someone else. It didn't feel right to become involved with someone without love.

"Wait," she said when he held up a hand to stop her. "Let me finish. John—I was right. I *can't* be involved with someone if I love someone else. I *can't* be involved with someone I don't love."

She waited for the interminable space of two seconds before she let him in on her biggest revelation of all. The one that had taken her almost two full weeks to believe. "That's why I know that I love you."

Very slowly, he turned his head, searched her face.

"I love you," she repeated. "I couldn't have made love to you if I didn't."

The horse barn could have fit inside the silence, it was so huge.

"Didn't see that one coming, did you?" she finally asked with a shaky laugh. "Well, if it's any consolation, neither did I."

He looked like he was ready to run. He looked cornered and trapped and like he was wishing he were anywhere she wasn't.

What he didn't look like was a man who was happy about her declaration.

"I don't know what to say to that," he said after another huge silence.

Well, it had been a long shot. And she'd had to get it out, had to see if he felt the same. Obviously, he didn't. Or at least he didn't want to and that was as much of a barrier as the Great Wall of China.

"Your face says it all, cowboy," she said with a sad smile. "Don't worry. It's okay. I don't expect anything in return."

"You should," he said, his eyes filled with an anger she didn't quite understand. "You should expect *everything*."

"Yes, well, we go with what we get, right? You were up-front from the beginning. You don't do serious relationships. The problem is, I do…and the irony is, you're the one who forced me to understand that.

"Goodbye, John," she said. "Don't worry. It won't get uncomfortable. I won't let it. Sundown's a small town. We'll be running into each other now and again and it will be okay. But I think it would be best if you got a different vet."

And then she left him.

It was over.

And life went on. She knew that better than anyone. Just like she knew about the pain of losing someone she loved.

He was relieved, that's what he was, John told himself over the next couple of weeks. Damn relieved that Ali had made it so easy for him. Hell, he was usually the one who ended things when he saw signs of a woman getting too involved, looking for more than he could give them. He'd been yelled at, bawled out, called everything but a son of God. But he'd never had a woman just walk away after she told him she loved him.

Ali loved him. At least she thought she did. She'd get over it.

And so would he.

That thought stopped him cold as he rode the fence line with Clive that afternoon. It wasn't that he was lonely. And he really didn't have anything to get over. At least he didn't until his brain latched on to a memory of Ali—smiling in the sun, whispering in the night, cooking dinner while he did any number of things to distract her.

Sure, he missed her company. That would fade soon enough. And life would get back to normal…at least as normal as his life got.

"What you got there?" he asked when he saw the old cowhand slow to a stop by a post.

"Hornets' nest," Clive said. "Oh, hell. It's a live one."

"Get the hell out of there," John yelled just as Clive

set spurs to the three-year-old gelding who was already a little spooky since this was his first time away from the herd.

It all happened so fast then that John could only watch in horrified silence. The green-broke gelding went berserk when the nest of hornets, riled by the scent of man, flew out to investigate. The horse bolted, bucking and crow-hopping across the range like a bronc. Clive rode him through the bucks, but then the gelding reared up on his back legs, then threw himself over backwards, landing on top of Clive.

Heart in his throat, John cued Snowy into a dead run to get to Clive. The gelding was on his feet and running hell-bent for the barn a good ten miles back when John reined in and flew to the ground.

"Oh, God," he swore when he saw the extent of the damages.

There was blood. A lot of it. On his head, below his knee.

"Hey, bud, you with me?"

Clive groaned then coughed, a convulsive, labored sound that ended in a wheeze that made John's face drain to pale.

Head injury. And a compound fracture—probably the tibia, he decided, as Clive's eyes fluttered shut. And if his suspicions were right, he also had some busted ribs—possibly a collapsed lung.

It was bad. Real bad.

He felt his head swim as all around him the world

went fuzzy, and the Montana foothills became the mouth of an Afghanistan cave in the dead of winter. And he couldn't stop the blood. His fingers were so cold…so was the leg he was working on. Cold and mangled as the young soldier cried for his mother…

Clive's clawlike grip on his arm snapped him back to the moment. "Can…can't b-breathe."

John shook himself out of the flashback. Set himself on autopilot. And did what he'd been trained to do.

Sweat was running off his face by the time he'd made an airway. Satisfied that Clive was breathing better, he pulled out his cell, dialed 911 and briefed the dispatcher on his location and Clive's condition.

"Hang on, you old coot," he whispered, covering Clive with Snowy's saddle blanket and checking the makeshift chest tube he'd had to insert using a pen casing he'd found in his saddlebag.

Then he went about the business of cutting off Clive's boot and seeing to his leg. What seemed like hours passed until he finally heard an ambulance approach, cutting across the pastureland, making its own path since the nearest road was two miles away.

He'd never been so relieved, or so surprised when in addition to a pair of paramedics, Ali jumped out of the vehicle and ran toward them.

Ali raced over to Clive and dropped to her knees at his side. She cut a quick look at John, read the question in his eyes.

"Dr. Lundstrum's out of town," she explained as she noted the paramedics examine the makeshift chest tube. "I heard the 911 call come in on the radio and asked to come along."

Mark Smith and the other paramedic, Jason Olson, prepared an IV drip.

Anguish and fear. Ali saw it all on John's face as he knelt by Clive's side and brought them up to speed on what he'd done.

Ali could hardly believe what she saw and heard him say. What looked like a nasty compound fracture was set and braced with leather straps—probably off a saddle—and what appeared to be the sole of a boot.

"You did this?" she asked.

At John's grim nod, she shook her head. "You probably saved his life." The paramedics eased Clive onto a gurney.

"These guys can handle it from here," she said, seeing the worry on John's face. "If you want to go with them, I'll take your horse back."

He shook his head.

She wanted to ask him how he'd known what to do but her questions would have to wait.

"Stay with him," John said. "Please."

"I'll wait with him until you can get to the hospital. Don't worry about him, John. He's tough. He's going to be fine. You saw to that."

Clive was going to be fine, the doctors at the E.R. in the Bozeman hospital assured her much later. It was going to be a difficult recovery, but he'd be okay after surgery. The adrenaline that had fueled her let down on a rush of relief. She couldn't wait for John to come so she could give him the good news.

Several hours passed, though, and he never showed up.

She finally went to the nurse's station. "Has there been a tall, good-looking cowboy in asking about an admit through E.R.? Clive Johnson?"

The charge nurse shook her head. "Not since I've been here. We did get a call asking about Mr. Johnson though. Said he was the old cowboy's boss."

"Did he say he was on the way in?"

"No. No, he just thanked me when I told him he was out of the woods and hung up."

"Hey, Doc."

Ali looked up to see Mark Smith walking toward the exit.

"We're heading back to Sundown. If you need a lift, the bus is leaving."

"Thanks. Give me a minute, okay? I want to take a quick peek at Clive, then I'll be ready to go."

He looked so fragile lying there, his weathered brown face in stark relief against the pristine white linens.

But he opened his eyes when he sensed her at his bedside. "Care...careless old f-fool," he managed in a hoarse whisper.

Ali leaned in close and smiled. "Tough old cowhand." She took his hand, squeezed it. "You'll be up and around in no time."

"J.T." he wheezed.

"Saved your life," she told him. "I'm sure he'll be in to see you soon."

The old man slowly shook his head. "Won't…won't come to no…hospital."

She was about to assure him that of course J.T. would come when the significance of his statement hit her.

Won't come to no hospital.

Why would a man who was clearly trained in medical trauma refuse to come to a hospital? Unless…oh, God. Why hadn't she seen it before? He was a veteran. One of many soldiers who had returned from the war on terror but unable to leave the terror behind them. Had he been in a military hospital? Or wait…he knew more than basic first aid. Had he *worked* in a military hospital?

Maybe she was reaching. She didn't think so. In fact, she was more sure of what she needed to do than she'd been sure of anything for a very long time.

"He may not be able to come," she assured Clive, "but that doesn't mean he doesn't want to."

He nodded. "Good…boy. He's a…good boy."

Yeah, she thought as Clive's rheumy old eyes closed and he fell back asleep. He's a good boy. And a better man. All he needed was a good woman to make him understand and believe.

Eleven

It was dark by the time Ali got back to Sundown. She took a quick shower, then drove out to the Tyler spread—and found it darker still inside the house when she pulled up in front of it. Not a single light burned from any window.

"John?" she called out softly after she'd rapped on the door several times. "Are you in there?"

When he didn't answer, she tried the doorknob. The door swung open to a house that was as quiet as it was dark. She flicked on the foyer light and thought she heard something at the end of the hallway that led to John's bedroom.

"John?"

Nothing.

Every instinct she owned told her he was in the house, more specifically, in his bedroom. She didn't bother to knock this time. She opened the door.

"Do not come in here."

His voice startled her, but she was a long ways from frightened. "Are you all right?" she asked, stepping farther into the room.

"I said, don't come in here."

She paused just inside the room. "Are you all right?" she repeated, recognizing from the hollow hardness in his voice that he was anything but all right.

"I'm fine."

"Yeah," she said, slowly. "You sound real fine. You want to tell me what's going on with you?"

"Just get the hell out of here, all right?"

"Actually, no. No, it's not all right," she said, reacting to the anger in his tone with stubborn determination. "And it's a little disconcerting conversing with a voice in the dark. Do you mind if I turn on a light?"

"I mind."

"Yeah, well, you know what? I don't care. But I do care about an old man all by himself in a hospital bed who could sure stand to see your face right about now."

"He knows why I'm not there."

"Well, good. That's good that he knows. Why don't you tell me so I'll know, too?"

All she got was silence.

She turned on the light.

And felt her heart break when she saw him on the bed.

This wasn't an angry man. This was a broken man. And the hollow, tortured look she saw in his eyes just before he rolled to his side and away from her brought tears to hers.

"Oh, sweetie." She rushed to the bed, hesitated for only a second at his clear attempt to shut her out, before she lay down behind him, curled her body around his and held on. Simply held on.

Long moments passed as she pressed herself against him, sharing her heat and her strength and an unwavering message that whatever it was, whatever was wrong, she was here for him. She wasn't going away.

She didn't know how long they lay that way, him silent and stiff as stone, her knowing instinctively that until he decided to start talking nothing she could say would make a difference.

Just when she thought she'd failed to penetrate whatever wall he'd erected between himself and the rest of the world, he rolled to his back and gathered her against him. Held her so tight tears stung her eyes at the sheer magnitude of his need.

"It's all right," she murmured. "It's all right. Let me. Let me make it better. Let me," she pleaded and started unbuttoning his shirt.

His hands stilled hers but she pushed them away. "Shhh. Just let me."

With slow, deliberate care, she undressed him, watched his face as she removed her own clothes. And then she joined him on the bed again, told him with her hands how much she loved him, showed him without words that he was everything.

He groaned and buried his hands in her hair when she bent over him, took him in her mouth and loved him until he was gasping her name.

By the time she was finished with him, all the tension had drained from his limbs. And when she snuggled up against him, nestling her nose into that inviting hollow against his throat, he hugged her hard. And then, blessedly, he started to talk.

John had never talked to anyone about what had happened in Afghanistan. Not the counselors when he returned home, not his navy buddies, not his folks. He'd never wanted anyone to be touched by the horror. And yet, he was telling Ali.

Everything. The grotesque aftermath of the wounded coming in from the front line. The villagers caught in the crossfire or blown to bits by the land mines planted by the Taliban. The dead and the dying. Terrified children with vacant eyes and bellies swollen from hunger.

He talked until he was hoarse. Wasn't aware that he was hanging on to her like she was the only thing holding him together. Wasn't aware of the tears flowing, of the weight of his experience easing, of her gentle encouragement and soft stroking hands.

Yet when he'd spent it all, all the memories, all the

horror, the flashbacks and the nightmares, even the shame over his inability to leave it behind and get on with his life, he was aware of a heavy weight having lifted off his shoulders, of a gnawing ache easing in his gut.

"You came back to Sundown to heal," she said when he'd lapsed into a silence like a calm after a storm. "In a way, so did I. Who knew that what we needed all along was each other."

He tipped her head back so he could see her eyes. Brushed the hair back from her forehead. "Yeah. Who knew?"

"You don't have to go through this on your own anymore. You know that, don't you? Please, tell me you won't shut me out. Not to protect me. Not to run away from me. Whatever ghosts haunt you, we'll face them together."

He looked deep into her eyes and the emotion she saw there stunned her. So did his actions when he laid her back on the bed and made slow, healing love to her. Telling her with deep kisses and whispered words that she was the only thing that mattered on this earth, giving himself over to her, giving in to the sensation of being totally and wholly consumed by her love.

And in his bed, where he'd once hidden in the dark, he let her take him into the light. He let go of his fear of intimacy, let go of his shame and confessed what he'd known deep down the first time he'd seen her.

"I love you," he whispered into her hair.

"I know," she whispered back, snuggled against his side and fell asleep, wrapped in the arms of love.

Epilogue

October in Sundown meant crisp, cool air, golden aspen and hard frosts past the upper foothills. It was anything but cold, though, as the town turned out to party at the Tylers' wedding reception at the Dusk to Dawn.

"I've got to tell you, J.T. This just does my heart a whole heap of good." Cutter, looking rakish and handsome in his black suit, clapped J.T. on the back, a broad grin lighting his face. "Watching the mighty fall. Man, what a sight. Brings a tear to my eye."

"He's been gloating ever since you popped the question," Peg put in, pretty in her mauve matron-of-honor dress. "I'm so happy for you, J.T.," she whispered, her eyes misty. "So very, very happy.

"And you," she said, turning to Ali and drawing her into a hug. "I just love saying I told you so. I did tell you he was perfect for you, didn't I?"

Ali laughed and returned Peg's warm embrace. "Yes. For the hundredth time, yes, you did. Thank you," she whispered and both of them fought back tears.

"Don't you dare start," Ali warned her friend, "Or I'll be blubbering, too."

"All right, you two." John tucked Ali under his arm and squeezed her tight. "Break it up or I'll have to separate you. There will be no crying today. That includes you, too, tough guy," he added giving Cutter a pointed look.

"In fact," he said, "I think I'd like to dance with my bride."

"Dance? Me? The woman with two left feet? Are you really sure about this?"

"Any excuse to get my hands on you," he said and drew her out onto the dance floor. Then, to the delight of everyone present, he scooped her up in his arms and started swaying to the music. "Work for you?"

She looped her arms around his neck. "It works." And then she kissed him.

The crowd broke into whoops of laughter and applause.

"I love you, Mrs. Tyler."

"And I love you. So do my parents. And my brothers."

"Still, it's got to be a shock for them."

"What? That I married a cowboy?"

"That and that you're a cradle-robbing hussy who

took advantage of my youth and naiveté to get me to marry you."

"Well, there is that. I plan on taking advantage of that youth tonight, cowboy. So don't wear yourself out dancing."

He let out a hoot of laughter. "Yes, ma'am. Whatever you say."

"I say I'm the luckiest woman on earth." And she kissed him again.

"What's a guy have to do to get a dance with the bride?"

Ali lifted her head to see Brett McDonald grinning at them.

"Get lost, McDonald. Find your own woman. This one's mine."

"Mac. Hi. I didn't see you earlier," Ali said, ignoring John's good-natured ribbing. "Thank you for coming."

"The pleasure's mine. Love to see a man bite the bullet and fall from the ranks of the perpetually single. Ali, you remember what I said now. Any time you want to dump this loser, I'm your man."

"Nice to know I've got a backup plan," she said, "but I'm not planning on needing it. As a matter of fact, I've got everything I need right here."

She'd never thought she would be able to say those words again. And yet, everything *was* here. She would always love David. She would never forget him. But this man…this man who had opened himself up to her when he'd let no one else in, was now her everything.

"What are you thinking so hard about?" he asked as he continued to hold her.

"About how lucky I am. And about leaving you."

The double take he did was so comical, she laughed.

"For him," she said, pointing to the corner of the room where Clive sat in his wheelchair glaring at Mable Clemmons who had taken it upon herself to see to his every need.

"I see your point. If ever a man needed rescuing, he does."

He became serious suddenly as he set her on her feet. Taking both of her hands in his, he brought them to his mouth. "And if ever there was a woman up to the task of saving lost men, it's you."

Her heart felt as though it would burst with the love she felt for this man. "I love you."

"That, darlin' girl, is something I'm going to hold you to forever."

* * * * *

DYNASTIES: THE ASHTONS

A family built on lies...
brought together by dark, passionate secrets.

This provocative family saga continues with

A RARE SENSATION
by Kathie DeNosky
(Silhouette Desire #1633)

Coming to Napa Valley to meet her new family,
Abigail Ashton isn't sure what to expect. She certainly
didn't dream of falling head over boot heels for the
rugged and sexy ranch foreman, Russ Gannon. Or
spending a night of mind-blowing passion in his bed.
Can Abigail make a lone wolf like Russ see that their
one-night stand could become something more?

Available at your favorite retail outlet.

If you enjoyed what you just read,
then we've got an offer you can't resist!

Take 2 bestselling love stories FREE!

Plus get a FREE surprise gift!

Clip this page and mail it to Silhouette Reader Service™

IN U.S.A.	IN CANADA
3010 Walden Ave.	P.O. Box 609
P.O. Box 1867	Fort Erie, Ontario
Buffalo, N.Y. 14240-1867	L2A 5X3

YES! Please send me 2 free Silhouette Desire® novels and my free surprise gift. After receiving them, if I don't wish to receive anymore, I can return the shipping statement marked cancel. If I don't cancel, I will receive 6 brand-new novels every month, before they're available in stores! In the U.S.A., bill me at the bargain price of $3.80 plus 25¢ shipping and handling per book and applicable sales tax, if any*. In Canada, bill me at the bargain price of $4.47 plus 25¢ shipping and handling per book and applicable taxes**. That's the complete price and a savings of at least 10% off the cover prices—what a great deal! I understand that accepting the 2 free books and gift places me under no obligation ever to buy any books. I can always return a shipment and cancel at any time. Even if I never buy another book from Silhouette, the 2 free books and gift are mine to keep forever.

225 SDN DZ9F
326 SDN DZ9G

Name	(PLEASE PRINT)	
Address	Apt.#	
City	State/Prov.	Zip/Postal Code

Not valid to current Silhouette Desire® subscribers.

Want to try two free books from another series?
Call 1-800-873-8635 or visit www.morefreebooks.com.

* Terms and prices subject to change without notice. Sales tax applicable in N.Y.
** Canadian residents will be charged applicable provincial taxes and GST.
All orders subject to approval. Offer limited to one per household.
® are registered trademarks owned and used by the trademark owner and or its licensee.

DES04R   ©2004 Harlequin Enterprises Limited

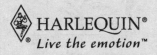

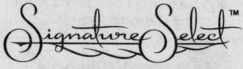
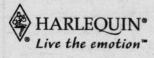

Coming in February 2005
from

Silhouette

Desire

Margaret Allison's
A SINGLE DEMAND
(Silhouette Desire #1637)

Cassie Edwards had gone to a tropical resort
to find corporate raider Steve Axon, but ended up
losing her virginity to a sexy bartender instead.
Cassie then returned home to a surprise:
her bartender *was* Steve Axon! Mixing business
with pleasure was not part of her plan, and
Cassie was determined to forget that night—
but Steve had another demand....

Available at your favorite retail outlet.

COMING NEXT MONTH

#1633 A RARE SENSATION—Kathie DeNosky
Dynasties: The Ashtons
Veterinarian Abigail Ashton wasn't looking to lose her virginity while staying at Louret Vineyards—then again, she hadn't counted on meeting sexy cowboy Russ Gannon. After a night of unexpected passion, Russ assumed he wasn't Abby's kind of guy. Little did he know, he'd caused a rare sensation that Abby didn't want to end.

#1634 HER MAN UPSTAIRS—Dixie Browning
Divas Who Dish
Marty Owens needed to remodel her home and asked handsome contractor Cole Stevens for help, never guessing their heated debates would turn into heated passion with one thing leading to another…and another…. Yet Marty knew that the higher she flew the harder she'd fall, and wondered if her heart could handle falling for the man upstairs.

#1635 BREATHLESS PASSION—Emilie Rose
The only son of North Carolina's wealthiest family, stunningly sexy Rick Faulkner needed Lily West's help. Before long, their platonic relationship turned into white-hot passion, and now Lily, a girl from the wrong side of the tracks, wanted her Cinderella story to last forever….

#1636 OUT OF UNIFORM—Amy J. Fetzer
Marine captain Rick Wyatt and his wife, Kate, were great together—skin to skin. But beyond the bedroom door, Rick closed Kate out emotionally, and she wanted in. When an injury forced Rick out of uniform, Kate passionately set out to win the battle for her marriage.

#1637 A SINGLE DEMAND—Margaret Allison
Cassie Edwards had gone to a tropical resort to meet with corporate raider Steve Axon but ended up losing her virginity to a sexy bartender instead. Then Cassie returned home to a surprise: her bartender *was* Steve Axon! Mixing business with pleasure was not part of her plan and Cassie was determined to forget that night—but Steve had another demand….

#1638 BOUGHT BY A MILLIONAIRE—Heidi Betts
Chicago's Most Eligible Bachelor, millionaire Burke Bishop, wanted a child and hired Shannon Moriarity to have his baby. Knowing that Burke would make a wonderful father, Shannon had agreed to keep things strictly business—but soon she realized Burke would make the perfect husband. But would Mr. Anti-Marriage agree to Shannon's change of terms?

SDCNM0105